OFFICINA
MARZIANI

36

THE CAVIAR LADY
Michele Marziani

ISBN 978-88-93372-20-6

ANTONIO TOMBOLINI
EDITORE

Via Villa Costantina, 61,
60025 Loreto Ancona
Italy

Translated from Italian by Anna Carruthers

Editing by Radici Translation and Wordcraft Ltd - Canada

email: info@antoniotombolini.com

www.antoniotombolini.com

Cover design by Marta D'Asaro
Page layout Marianna Mordenti

MICHELE MARZIANI

THE CAVIAR LADY

historical fiction

ANTONIO TOMBOLINI EDITORE

In memory of Domenico Tommaso Marziani,
my grandfather, station master

1

"A whopper! A whopper!" The cries go up and all of a sudden there are children streaming excitedly along the main embankment. I jump on my bike and pedal along to catch up with them.

"Who caught it? Whose is it?" I question them urgently.

"The Turk, it's the Turk's," they shoot back, hardly pausing for breath. Amelia who grows hay for rabbits shouts over: "What are you lot doing going to the Turk's house? You know he's got no family."

"He's got his niece now," the children reply breathlessly, and when they run you can almost hear their labored breathing interspersed with the sound of their clogs: "A whopper! A whopper!"

The blur of criss-crossing legs flashing along the embankment soon attracts the attention of other children weeding the vegetable patches by their homes or mending the nets, who rush to join us. Their muscles are not tired and they race to overtake the others, because only the first to deliver the news gets the reward, the coin. The others can expect a piece of bread if they're lucky. But not from the Turk, now Bechi lives there. Now that's the house we all like best: because apart from the coin there are barley sugar sweets for everyone. Sweets you suck slowly, carefully, praying they'll last forever. Mario and the other children say there's never been anything like it among the fishing families. But the Turk comes from the East, they always say, respectfully. He's not really like us.

And it's long-legs Mario who puts on a sprint finish and gets to the Turk's house first, pulling up short at the last minute and almost falling over his feet, stirring up a cloud of dust with his clogs. He's beating on the door with his fists when the others rush up yelling. Bechi opens, smiling. Mario looks at her but has no breath, or strength, left to speak.

"A whopper! A whopper!" shout the others, piling in behind him, pushing and jostling to get to the front, to be in his place, mouths open showing teeth, pulling at each other's sweaters and jackets. Mario catches his breath, swallows and blurts out:

"We don't know if it's a female, but it's big, really big. The others had to help him get it in the boat. Nicola almost fell in the river, the Turk was all red and swearing every time he pulled up the net..."

Bechi smiles. I peek at her and I think she looks like a fairy queen: what does she care about how they caught the sturgeon? No-one even knows where she's from, I remind myself. All that counts is the money: one fish, if it's really that big, will see you through the season. Bechi sees me and gives me a little wave:

"Hi Nellino!"

"Hi Bechi!"

She tells the children to wait, then goes back into the house. She returns with the coin and barley sugar sweets for everyone. There's never been anything like this here before, down on the riverside among the fishing families. I set off again and pedal furiously along the embankment: I have to see the look on Nicola's face. I cross paths with the boat on its way back to the riverside. Oh my goodness it really is big: I can see it from here on the bank. It's lying in the middle of the boat with its tail sticking up out of the net they've put over it to keep it still. The Turk puts a piece of wet sack cloth over its head so it can't see, to stop it from thrashing out with its tail. Then just to make sure, he leans over it with his body, to stop it jumping out of the boat. He looks like a mother protecting her child, that's the image that springs to my mind. But really it's just a fish, a sturgeon. The god of fish, that's what the Turk calls them, but everyone knows he's not exactly a good Catholic.

Nicola rows to the shore and shouts over to me:

"Hey Mr. Perfect! If you don't mind getting those white hands of yours dirty, run to my house and get two ropes so we can tie it to the pole, then go and tell your uncle."

"So, it's a female?"

"Oh yes Adam, there aren't any males as big as this in the Po River..."

It took me a while to figure out why the Turk calls me Adam. It means "man" in the language of the Turks. He told me the night I plucked up the courage to ask. He calls me a man, but always with that half smile so it's like he really means mummy's boy. But he calls me Adam all the same, at least when I have to learn something. Otherwise it's Nello. Nellino is what everyone else calls me, but the Turk hardly ever does.

I like it when he calls me Adam, but there's not much that's manly about me: I'm nearly twelve, in short trousers and my Fascist Youth uniform with the black shirt. It's Saturday, the

Fascist Saturday dedicated to the character-building activities of the youth movement. If I really was a man and not a boy I would be in the Militia Corps, even if my Uncle wouldn't like it. And the Turk probably doesn't either. Maybe it's not really my kind of thing anyway, seeing that instead of going to the rally in the village I'm here tying up the fish in the stretch of river in front of the Turk's house.

"This'll take us right through to the autumn if the river doesn't carry it off," decrees the Turk, spitting on the ground. "No doubt it would have been easier if we'd caught it on a Monday. Now we need to keep watch and make sure it stays alive till the errand boy gets here..."

"Doesn't the caviar Lady come herself anymore?" I ask.

"No, not at the moment, I mean, I don't think she'll be coming for a while..." stutters the Turk, momentarily losing the quiet self-containment that lends him dignity even when he has sweat running down his forehead and his hands are all cut from the sturgeon's scutes, his hair is damp with water from the Po and all sticking up, and his clothes are so threadbare and filthy he looks like a beggar. But there's something noble in his bearing, in his whole approach to fishing. He's different from everyone else down here on the riverside, it's probably something to do with his name, the Turk. I'm probably too young to put my finger on it exactly. I'm not really Adam, I'm just little Nellino.

"If you want I'll come and help guard the sturgeon," I say, to make myself useful.

"Yes, and in that get-up you'll soon have it standing to attention," the Turk laughs, and I feel awkward in my uniform even though I really like it.

I wear it for my country, for the heirs of Rome. We are all Italian and we are all Fascists. Well, almost all of us are. Mother definitely isn't, because of my father who went off and got himself killed in Spain. Uncle I'm not sure, because when the Federal Secretary comes to the station, or the squads pass by on their way to a parade, he puts on his black shirt to blow the whistle and hold up the signaling disk, but when we're supposed to gather in the square to listen to the radio through the big speakers to hear the Duce's speeches, he always has something else to do. And when he speaks to the Turk he uses the old "*lei*" form of address, not "*voi*" like Mussolini wants us to.

But I'm just a boy, and like he says, children shouldn't go poking their noses into certain things. I don't think the Turk is a good patriot either, a good Fascist, he's from too far away. He only deals with sturgeons anyway. But me and his son Nicola are friends, we went to school together. He had to leave at the end of primary school: the Turk needed a hand in the boat and Nicola's mother died giving birth to him. When Nicola was little the Turk managed by paying a deckhand, but after elementary school it was time for Nicola to start pulling his weight.

I tell Nicola about what we're doing in history and geography when we're out hunting for duck eggs or fishing for frogs. And now of course there's his cousin Bechi, who came to live here a few months ago. Her parents died and she almost ended up with the nuns. That would have been a shame because she's really pretty. I know, I'm still young to be saying this, but when I watch her doing the housework I sometimes feel my pecker stirring in my pants. It's nothing to be ashamed of: a good Fascist is supposed to be virile. That's what Orlando always says and his dad's in the Militia Corps so he knows about these things. Bechi, as well as being pretty, arrived with a whole trunk full of books that she keeps in the tool shed, behind the nets. Nicola showed me: at least he'll have the chance to read and, as Uncle says, further his education.

II

In the village everyone respects the Turk, but down on the riverside, by the bridge, among the fisherman, he's a genuine institution. Uncle says that on the Po the Turk has more clout than the priest in church. Not only because he can read and write and comes from far away, but because he knows about all the different kinds of sturgeon and can tell which ones to sell to make money on and which ones are not worth much. If the Turk takes a sturgeon to the broker or auctioneer he comes back with good money and keeps nothing back for himself. He knows if it's the size of fish that city folk like to eat, and takes it to the restaurant.

Mr. Otello, the owner of the restaurant, who never mixes with the people from the riverside, willingly comes down from upstairs to do business with the Turk. Mr. Otello only buys sturgeon from the Turk, and sends the other fishermen packing - he says they're time-wasters who can't tell a tiddler from a sturgeon. That's what people say about the Turk, though others remember that when he arrived people gave him a wide berth. There were already thirty sturgeon boats belonging to the fishermen who lived on the riverside and when the Turk turned up he didn't look like he was used to hard work, with that blonde wife of his, who Mario's father says couldn't even speak Italian. They came here and bought a house, just like that. It was easy to buy a house in 1917, all the men were away fighting in the war and the houses on the riverside were empty, so it was no problem if you had the money. The Turk made a song and dance about it but I reckon that he did have money. When Mario's dad tells the story he lights a cigarette, a cigarette that stinks, it's not even tobacco. Then he puffs out the smoke, coughing. He likes it when I ask about the Turk, because like everyone else round here he respects him, but I think he's a bit envious of him too, so he likes talking about him, especially if he has a bottle of wine in front of him.

"You're young," he says, "but in those days everyone was away fighting in the war, and there was so much poverty here you could cut it with a knife and serve it up for dinner. I only stayed behind because of my leg." He looks down at his twisted foot, that makes him hop and jump when he walks, but doesn't stop him from hoisting sturgeons into his boat. Quinto, Mario's father, is a great fisherman, I've seen him pulling in sturgeons that weigh almost a hundred kilos and lifting them up by himself on the harpoon. Then again, he wants Mario to go to school so he goes out in the boat with his wife who's all skinny and doesn't have enough strength in her arms to hoist up the big fish.

"To cut a long story short," he continues, "at first we didn't like the Turk. We were sure he was hiding something. The Great War had just finished and the police went to talk to him, but all his papers were in order so they couldn't say anything. Then the whole thing with the music started and we all thought he was a bit touched in the head. Him and his wife, a fine woman she was that's for sure, nothing like our wives. She had eyes as blue as ice, golden hair like wheat and alabaster skin. Her arms were strong and shapely, and what legs! When she stood in the stern she looked like a captain. The Turk was always proud when he called her name. I still remember it: "Lukina, Lukina!' I don't know where she got a name like that, though..."

"And the music?"

"Ah yes, before the Turk showed up no-one played music to catch sturgeon, not like it is now with people paying bands to play on their boats. No, back then we would just put down our nets, and pass them along, and if we got something, fine and good. If not, we would just have to queue up behind the other boats and wait our turn to pass along again."

"Yes, but the music?"

"Be patient, I'm coming to that."

Mario's father pours himself another glass of wine, leaving me on tenterhooks. I wish he'd get on with it because Mother will probably be waiting for me by now. But I have to know about the Turk, because he's Nicola's father, because he's strange, and because I came here on purpose to find out. When Mother gets cross with me she says I'm as nosey as an old woman.

"And the music?"

"Well, he sorted out his house in that funny way of his, with roses around the vegetable patch and by the door. Then he started working on the boat. He didn't ask any of us for any help, he got it looking spick and span all by himself. And the nets too, they were all tangled, and he bought the hemp and knotted it himself. He had money for hemp when the rest of us were dirt poor." Mario's father spits on the ground again, enviously.

"We wouldn't have helped him anyway," he continues, taking breath. "We were scared of him, he wasn't one of us, even though he says he comes from who knows what village on the Po, in the Delta. He mentions it from time to time but I can't remember the name and it's probably not even true. Anyway, spring comes round and he and his wife put the boat in the river. Now we'll have to wait even longer to pass our nets, we all think. More mouths to feed. And people who aren't even from around here. But in the end the Turk fed us all, there's no two ways about it, he looked after us all. He knew we didn't like him so he didn't fish with us but went further downstream, where the river bed wasn't dredged, so he risked his nets every time he went out. But then of course he didn't pass his nets along the river bed, so there was no way they would get caught on something.

He would stand with his boat across the current, then get out his *ocarina* and start playing. Then his wife would shout: "There it is! There it is!"

And he would put down the ocarina and pull in the net. That year the Turk caught more than anyone else. We tried putting the evil eye on him, but for the whole of the season he always came back to shore with a sturgeon. He would play his ocarina and catch fish, just like that. And when the buyer came the Turk would bargain with him, man to man, not just looking at his feet like the rest of us. He would talk and argue his point and hold his arms out. You could see he knew what he was talking about. We're just simple folk Nellino, and that's why we're still living like beggars on the riverside."

And he pauses again to spit, smoke and fill his glass.

"And then what?"

"And then in the get-togethers on the long summer nights there would be talk of burning his house down, sinking his boat and..."

"And what?"

"No, these are not things for children's ears."

"Tell me what."

"No, you'd go straight to hell."

"You'll go if I tell your wife that instead of mending the nets you're here drinking and talking to me..."

"You dirty scoundrel!"

"I was only joking."

"Show more respect to your elders."

"Yes, of course." I lower my eyes.

"Well, we thought we'd have some fun with the Turk's wife, you know what I mean?"

I don't really, but I pretend I do and keep on with my questions.

"So did you do it?"

"No! The priest, not Don Antonio, but the old one, Don Armando, brought us to our senses. He called us a bunch of ignorant heathens and told us that if the Turk was catching more fish than us then it was up to us to learn how to do it, and what was all this talk of burning down people's houses. So the next spring two of us took it in turns to go and spy on the Turk instead of going fishing, until he noticed what we were up to and came to speak to Anselmo, the oldest fisherman - Pietro's grandfather, you know who I mean."

I nod, of course I know him, but I wish Mario's father

would get on with it, because they're bound to be waiting for me at home and I don't want my ears pulled for being late.

"Well, the Turk went to see Anselmo to say that there was no need to spy on him, and that if we wanted to learn his way he would teach us. So we got together one evening to decide what to do. Some people were against it, and reckoned that he wasn't a real fisherman. Others thought we should give it a try and see what he had to say. In the end we decided to put him to the test, so we invited him down to Nena's tavern. It was just us fishermen in the tavern that night. We put a big bottle of grappa down in front of him and start pouring. It was a big thing for us, paying for all that grappa, but we had to see whether he was one of us. So we keep pouring out the grappa and knocking it back, holding up our glasses and shouting 'Down the hatch!' And he drinks and drinks, and never says a word. Till Anselmo says: 'So what is it with the music?'

And the Turk tells us that fish like music, and that he uses his ocarina to attract the sturgeon. He says that in other places they use whole orchestras, violins, trombones, the lot. So Anselmo says: 'You mean people fish for sturgeon in other places?'

And the Turk bursts out laughing.

'Astrakhan,' he says. 'Astrakhan is the capital of sturgeon and beautiful women and caviar.'

'But what about Ferrara?' says Toni. 'And Pila? And Milan?' ask the others.

We all want to know more, so the Turk starts telling us about fish six meters long, measuring it out in paces across the tavern floor, fish with a hundred kilos of caviar in them, and the fishermen renting boats with musicians to catch them. The whole thing sounds crazy to us.

'And just where would this Astrakhan be?'

'On the Caspian Sea, in Russia, near the land of the Turks.'

He draws a map of the world, but what do we know, for us even Ferrara is miles away. Or Milan, where no-one from round here has ever been. Some of us have left the riverside, but only to go to the war, in Libya, or on the Carso plateau, or along the Piave and Tagliamento rivers, but no-one's ever seen a river bigger than the Po. None of us had seen sturgeons anywhere else.

Well, he'd almost made us come round that night, but Toni wasn't having any of it and shouted over:

'You're not a fisherman, you're a devil!'

It might have been the grappa talking - or maybe it just wasn't very good grappa - but then he got up on the table too. Nena yelled at him to get down but he yelled louder and pointed at the Turk, shouting,

'If you're a fisherman you know what it takes to get the biggest sturgeon... Go on then, tell us, if you can.'

He was ranting away, looking at us as if to say 'Now I've got him. He's not one of us, he's the devil, Beelzebub, and even Don Armando will have to face it. People like him deserve to be burned here on earth, without waiting for hell.'

So the Turk got to his feet, and with the grappa he looked taller, and he smiled - he had all his teeth, like a proper gentleman - and he said: 'A white horse is worth just as much on the Po as it is in Astrakhan.'

No-one said a word or moved a muscle, then Anselmo went up to him and spat on the palm of his hand, and the Turk did the same and they shook hands. Toni started hollering again, still standing on the table, but no-one was heeding him any more. We opened the old wine, a bottle that Nena was keeping for a special occasion.

That's how it went. After that he fitted in with us, or rather we fitted in with him, because he's the one who can talk about fish, he knows about selling, about doing deals on caviar, about what music the band has to play. We were all sorry when Lukina died giving birth to Nicola. All the women, our women, helped out when he was little. A father can't do it on his own."

So there it was. Now I knew. Apart from one thing.

"But why is he called the Turk if he comes from Russia?"

"How should I know? The furthest I've been is Ferrara!" Mario's father replies, laughing.

III

But the question keeps going round and round in my head till I work up the courage to ask the Turk why everyone calls him that. I don't know what kind of answer I'll get, after Mario's father's stories. But he's in the mood to chat and he tells me he was once the gardener at the villa in Tarabya, the summer home of the Italian Ambassador to Istanbul.

"A gardener? But how do you know everything about sturgeons then?"

"Because fish need looking after, just like roses."

I don't know what to say: I don't have a clue what he's talking about.

I started to figure some things out one day when something strange happened at home. It was Sunday and Uncle wanted us all there for lunch in the station. Meaning not just Mother and me, but also the Turk and Nicola. Bechi wasn't around back then. The table was set with bread and butter and a bottle of Malvasia wine that Uncle got sent by train.

"This might not be embassy champagne," said Uncle. "But if you're talking caviar ours is second to none. Just taste this."

We were flabbergasted, the Turk started saying that he wouldn't dream of it, no way, but Uncle insisted.

"It comes from the Lady, it's a present. We could have sold it but I thought it was only right to share it."

The Turk started up again, but then he gave in. And his eyes lit up, he even kissed Mother on the hand. He took out a little pouch with a tiny gleaming white spoon. It was in the pocket of his jacket. I saw him looking for it.

"I hope you don't mind," he said.

And he began picking the caviar off the butter and placing it slowly in his mouth using the shiny spoon, one egg at a time, almost as if he was taking holy communion. He closed his eyes and you could tell it wasn't his first taste of caviar, and his thoughts were far far away. For us it was the first time, and for Uncle and Mother, as far as I know, it was the last.

But the whole gardener story began to sound a bit suspect to me so I started spending more time with Nicola, because he was my friend, and to get the chance to bombard him with questions. Who was the Turk? Just who was his father? At the time I was reading Salgari's books and felt like I was pretty well versed in all things exotic, and ready to uncover this mystery.

IV

As for me, and what I have to do with the sturgeon fishing, well, I am the official messenger, because I have a bicycle and Uncle is the stationmaster. I like it because in the village people know who I am: I've heard people saying: "You know, Nellino, the boy who brings word of the sturgeon." I like my name Nellino and also my surname, Scaramagli. And the fact that I live in the station with Uncle Pompeo and Mother, whose name is Argia.

I am the stationmaster's nephew, so I am quite important in the village, perhaps more due to that than the sturgeons, and it means I get to wander around among the locomotives, go to the farm supplies store, and Remo's house. Remo is the signalman who lives right by the rails. From there in one hop you're in front of the signal box, the front door of which faces the railway, rather than the street, which is behind it. Remo doesn't know anyone who would come in from the street anyway. As Uncle always says, we're railwaymen, we know the score.

V

72 kilos Stop Female Stop Await arrival station Stop.

"What about the greeting? And the sender? You never put anything in these telegrams and people will get the wrong idea and think it's the post mistress who's rude."

"But this is all my Uncle said to put... Look here..." And I show her the hand-written note.

The telegraph operator smiles. But then she grumbles: "I don't understand why you can't use the telegraph in the station. Why do you need to come to the post office?"

I just shrug my shoulders but really I know the answer: the telegraph in the station is for official railway business, it's not something public for all and sundry to use. Uncle often says that. He would never use it. And when the caviar Lady comes we give her the receipt for what we spent on the telegram and she always pays us back, right down to the last cent.

Actually she hasn't come for a while - her errand boy has been coming. His name is Girolamo but we all just call him the errand boy. He came a few times with the Lady and she called him Gino. He's tall and a bit podgy, and he's always out of breath when he gets off the train. He has fat fingers and he sweats like you wouldn't believe. I've never seen anyone sweat so much. He takes his jacket off and his shirt is always soaking wet under the arms.

When he has to hold a fish he opens the top button of his shirt and his tie, and his neck looks like it's about to explode. Sweat starts trickling down his forehead. He hasn't got much hair, which maybe is why you can see the sweat so much. Anyway he looks like a pig, I mean a nice, kind pig, not the sort you'd gladly butcher for the Feast of Saint Anthony.

He smiles a lot, but doesn't say much. He puts ice into the zinc case, his own personal one, or rather the Lady's one, places the egg sac inside it, seals it shut, says goodbye and goes outside, where he sits on the concrete bench on the platform to wait for the train. As if he was a complete stranger. He lights a cigarette, smokes and adjusts his glasses.

When he cuts open a sturgeon his glasses always slide down his nose because of the sweat. The errand boy is a funny person, but we like him, because the Lady sends him, and because he's not afraid of hard work, or at least that's what Mother always says.

But when the Lady came it was different. She traveled in third class but behaved as if she were in first, and she would get off the train and greet everyone and we would all stand to attention. Uncle would invite her into the station for a coffee, which he always manages to get hold of because Remo the signalman has a sort of shop in his house where you can get practically anything. It costs a bit more, but you can get anything there, even things which aren't always available. And I would run hell for leather along the drainage channel to the main embankment, to shout down to the riverside: "The Lady's here!" "The Lady's here!" Everyone knew it was the caviar Lady.

VI

When I tell the Turk the errand boy is here he pulls the fish out of the water where it's tied like a dog on a leash, and knocks it out. You have to know how to do it properly, because you want the fish to be still but it's better if it stays alive - it's better to finish it off in the station. If it's a small one you can put it in a bag, like a priest in a robe, and tie it to the crossbar of the bicycle. In that case the Turk tells me to get off my bike, then ties the sturgeon tight to the crossbar and sends me back to the station.

"As fast as you can," he always says.

Which is hardly necessary: class of '28 I am, I've good muscles in my legs and a great set of lungs on me. I could be Bartali's wingman, no problem. Well, not really, but sometimes I imagine myself there, racing along, like you see in the illustrations in *La Domenica del Corriere* Sunday paper. I can see myself winning, lifting my arms up without falling off because it's something I can do: I can also pedal with one foot, if need be. But sometimes there's a really big one, a gigantic fish that takes two men, even three to get it up out of the water and even the Turk's mallet is not enough to stun it. So he wraps it up tightly in bags, props its head over the handlebars of his bike, and ties it with a rope that goes through its gills and out of its mouth, with a double knot near the brakes and at the front near the light. Then he puts another bag over the saddle, places the fish on top and ties it to the crossbar with straps. The tail sticks out the back, over the mudguard and the Turk pushes the bike along, using one foot to turn the pedals to get to the station faster. For the smaller fish, by the time he gets to the station the Lady or the errand boy are already doing their business.

Mother always invites the Lady into the house, where we live, above the station. In the kitchen there's a table with a marble top that always looks too big when Mother is cooking, but always seems a bit small when the Lady or the errand boy put the fish down on it, ask if they can wash their hands and then cut its belly open. The sturgeon always quivers at first, but then it stops moving. Then right after that the Turk kills it. Every time he says: "It's suffered enough for us," like he really cares about the fish.

Remo's wife used to come and clean up because it's a dirty job getting the eggs out. Now Bechi comes, which means I can see her and we can talk. It just doesn't seem right to see her there, her being just a girl and all, not much more than a child really, on her hands and knees cleaning up blood from our kitchen floor.

"Let me give you a hand," I say.

I get down on my knees beside her. She lifts her eyes, which are black, but not that dull black like the girls round here. Her eyes are bright and they sparkle, they are big, round and kind. I don't really know what I'm trying to say, just that they're beautiful. She brushes her hair off her forehead. Just a strand.

"Thank you," she says.

She lowers her eyes. I can feel my face getting hot. I lean on the cloth but the floor is wet and the cloth slides away, leaving me face down in the sturgeon's blood. Mother sees me and bursts out laughing. Bechi joins in too. And Uncle, who hasn't said a word, looks at me pityingly and says:

"That'll teach you to do women's work. Leave the kitchen to them."

Once the egg sac has been taken out the Turk slices up the sturgeon. After it's been emptied it's not always easy to sell the fish whole. If it still looks okay he gets me to call the factor and does the deal right there, in the kitchen, until Mother shoos them all away. If it's a fish that can be sold whole the factor has us put it in one of the railway's zinc trunks and writes the address in Milan where it has to be sent. The money arrives by telegram in the station. The telegram says how much it is, then the money gets sent to the post office. In this case the telegram comes to the station because it's part of the rental of the zinc trunk.

VII

I've never met anyone quite so precise about everything. The Lady makes a perfect cut down the fish's belly with a knife called a scalpel. She looks at the egg sacs to see how big they are then pays. The Turk never haggles over the price with her. He just takes the money and says thank you. She apologizes to Mother for the trouble, smiles at me in a kind way and then goes down into Uncle's office. They always spend some time chatting before the first train to Ferrara comes along. I'd give anything to know what they talk about. I see them from behind the glass door in the station. Uncle always smiles when he talks to the Lady, but she doesn't move her mouth much, except to smoke, and she keeps the caviar box on the desk. It's her own personal box, not the station one, and it's always spotless. And so is she: not so much as a drop of blood on her, never a button undone, a hair out of place or a hint of sweat. She couldn't be more different from the errand boy. And she doesn't smell of fish, but violets. Her hands are long and quite wrinkly, a worker's hands, but her fingers are delicate and her nails always look perfect. So many times I've watched her cutting a sturgeon or holding her cigarette between her forefinger and middle finger. Uncle always holds his cigarette between his thumb and forefinger. I like watching them. And I'd like to know what they talk about but from the outside you can't hear anything and if Uncle sees me hanging around he sends me off on some errand or other.

When the train bell starts ringing they go out onto the platform together, Uncle and the caviar Lady. He puts his hat on, the hat that makes him look like a sailor, a sea captain like the ones in my comic *Il Vittorioso*. When the Lady isn't here he hardly ever puts his hat on to blow the whistle. He gets his signaling disk and whistle and then kisses her on the hand. I reckon it's a bit over the top. But I think that Uncle misses the Lady now she doesn't come any more. And he never invites the errand boy, whose box always seems to be a bit leaky, into his office. And maybe the errand boy wouldn't even go. In any case he never has anything to say for himself and he likes to wait on the platform. Of course the caviar season is in the spring, which here on the Po is the best season of all – the fog disappears after dawn, and the mosquitoes don't come out till nearer the summer.

VIII

Me and Nicola are friends starting from our names. Nellino and Nicola. At school the other kids are jealous and shout, "N and N, nobody's children." Because both of our names begin with N and both of us are orphans. I've got no father, Nicola no mother. We really are nobody's children. After a bit we got used to it and now it's almost a badge of honor because me and Nicola are unbeatable in the times tables and leapfrog and learning poems off by heart. I think it's a real shame that Nicola can't come to school any more. Because he came top out of the whole school in the fifth grade tests. Half the village went to try and convince the Turk to keep him at school. Uncle went, and even the teacher did too.

"There's more than enough for him to learn here," says the Turk.

"But he could really go far," insists the teacher.

Even the Federal Secretary has taken the matter to heart. We wrote him a letter and he comes down to the riverside in his car one afternoon with some Fascist soldiers.

"A good Italian like your son could serve his country and the party."

"Take a look around," says the Turk. "Just take a look:

earth, water and mud. This is our life. This is who we are."

The Turk isn't afraid of anyone. Which is probably why everyone is afraid of him.

"I can't afford to let Nicola go to school, I don't have any help on the boat and life is hard."

"But the teacher says he's the best in the village, and our country needs the best men."

"Let the country support him then."

"Don't you trust our Duce?"

"Of course I trust him, I just can't afford to send Nicola away to school."

And he looks him straight in the eye. The Federal Secretary turns abruptly and says that he will write to Rome. Then he gets to his feet. And his entourage gets up too. I look out of the window, outside the house. The Turk raises his arm: "*Saluto al Duce*!"

"*A noi*!" they fire back.

They turn on their heels and off they go.

The teacher doesn't fare any better. We see her coming on her bike. She never comes here, so we all go to greet her.

"Your father has to understand that a boy like you simply must continue his education."

Nicola doesn't say a word.

"I'll take you to him if you want."

Of course she wants to see the Turk: she's come out here on purpose. It's summer and the air is thick with mosquitoes.

"Father! Father!" calls Nicola.

The Turk comes out of the shed where he keeps his nets.

"Good evening."

"Good evening. I've come to talk to you about Nicola."

"I think I know why you're here, even the Fascists have been, but I just can't. I'm on my own. And why does he need to study to be a fisherman anyway? Spending a life time eating roots so that others can eat caviar."

"So it's true you've studied," the teacher lets slip. "You talk like a..."

"Subversive?" suggests the Turk.

"You shouldn't say that word!" she admonishes him.

He smiles, and lets out a laugh; she lowers her eyes. Nicola and I are awestruck: Nicola's father has made the teacher blush! The very teacher who's a sergeant major in class, who makes us all jump to our feet and stand to attention to sing the national anthem, recite the poems of Giosuè Carducci and repeat the names of the heroes of the Risorgimento and the Kings of Rome. Nicola's father laughs and she doesn't know where to look.

"Listen to me," he says, using the old "lei" form of address. "We don't need book learning to get by here."

Uncle tries to convince the Turk too. I think he even offers Nicola a job in the station.

"I've no help on the boat and Nicola is all I've got. Sending him to school would mean losing him," the Turk says to Uncle. "And we're here to stay."

Uncle insists: "At least the trade school!"

"Nicola already has a trade," replies the Turk.

So Uncle pats Nicola on the back and gives me a nudge:

"We'd better be on our way. This man is as stubborn as a mule."

"And right with it!" the Turk shoots back.

What Nicola misses about school are the books, but not all that time sitting at a desk.

"Now that I'm second in command I have a trade," he says every time I try to set him against the Turk.

"What about you? You've no trade."

"Oh yes I do. I go to school. And I'm the messenger for the sturgeons."

IX

I want to be a doctor when I grow up, I know it would make Uncle happy. And Mother.

"Who knows how many sick people you'll cure," she says to me sometimes, passing the kitchen table while I'm doing my homework, the same table where the sturgeons are gutted.

To be honest I'm not that bothered about the sick people, just the gig. Because Dr. Girardi used to have a gig that looked like a racing buggy and he toured the countryside in it visiting his patients. He would stop off at the station to play cards with Uncle, and have a glass of wine and a slice of salami. They would sit in the stationmaster's office downstairs and Dr. Girardi would offer Uncle one of his long cigars. Before the war he sometimes brought us a goose or capon that Mother would roast: what a feast! I was allowed to invite Nicola, but if it was sturgeon season he wouldn't come. Then, it was before 1940, Dr. Girardi swapped his gig for a car, a great big Isotta Fraschini it was, and at the same time he swapped his smile for a sense of superiority. He began to like his drink a bit too much and his patients didn't give him geese and capons any more, because he began running them over himself, or so people in the village used to say. One time he came in, belching, and wanted to come up into the apartment. Then he said some not very nice things to Mother, and Uncle took him by the arm and offered to take him back to his villa. But he turned round and his breath smelled of wine and garlic and he winked at Uncle and said: "I know you have dealings with Jews, but it won't go on forever, you mark my words."

And it didn't, at least not for Dr. Girardi, because he crashed his Isotta Fraschini. He went off the road and was found dead, something had crushed him and he suffocated. I don't know what it was exactly. Partly because I wasn't there – it was Uncle who told me about it – and partly because I don't think I'm really cut out to be a doctor.

"That car was too big for these roads," Uncle comments darkly.

"And just how does a country doctor come to get a car like that?" Mother adds.

"Everyone knows it was a present for some favors he did for the right people," Pasquina lets slip.

Pasquina is Remo's wife, who still sometimes comes to our house to clean.

And it has to be said, everyone was taken aback when he swapped his gig for the Isotta Fraschini. Some people said it was second hand, probably a payment for some gambling debt or who knows what. What I always remember is the last time he spoke to Uncle. That word, Jews, is a bad word. There can hardly be Jews here. Jews have big noses, they are heavy-set, wicked and tight-fisted. Riff raff. I know everything there is to know about the Jews, I read it in *The Defense of the Race* magazine.

We are Italian, Aryans. Anyone can see we're Aryans:

Mother is blonde, and beautiful. And when she puts her hair up you can see she's got knock-out blue eyes. Her eyes sparkle, her skin is pale with tiny, almost invisible freckles. All of us Scaramagli have them. I looked it up: it's an Aryan trait. In our family we're so blonde we could be mistaken for Germans. Well, not me and Uncle, we're a bit reddish to tell the truth, but only slightly. To be on the safe side, every so often Mother puts this smelly stuff on my hair. She says it's to keep lice away, but after she does it my hair is always a bit lighter than before. In any case race is important and I'm glad I'm Aryan and Italian because I've been through enough already what with having an anarchist and traitor to the homeland for a father. At home though, no-one ever talks about race, or anarchists, or the homeland.

At school, on the other hand, Mario and Vittorio always give me a hard time.

"A fisherman's son and the chemist's son! Cruelty makes no distinction between social classes then. They should be ashamed of themselves!" Mother exclaims, disgusted, when I ask her why Father betrayed our Country and why they call me a traitor. And Nicola a foreigner. Nobody's children, that's us.

X

Now I have to go to school by myself. I have to take the train to Ferrara, where nobody knows me or anything about me. Now race has become really important and at middle school I am held up as an example of the perfect Aryan. Put that in your pipe and smoke it, Mario and Vittorio. But my father really was a traitor.

"An idealist," says Mother.

"But following the wrong ideal," Uncle silences her.

In any case, right or wrong, he followed his idea and couldn't care less about me and Mother. She says that he did hold me in his arms a few times, and that there's even a picture of us somewhere. But I don't recall ever seeing him. I know his face, but only from a photograph. He went and got himself killed in Spain where Italy sent soldiers too. Only he was on the wrong side, with the anarchists and Bolsheviks.

"All you can do for him," says Don Antonio when I talk about him in confession, "is pray for his soul, even though he doesn't deserve it. People like him killed priests and shot at the Holy Sacraments. He was an animal, your father. Just as well you don't take after him. You are a good person, like your poor mother. A sign that the Lord God is merciful. *Ego te absolvo...*" Etcetera, etcetera.

I don't even have my father's surname, why should I feel bad about anything? What's it got to do with me?

"Love is blind, and people can make mistakes," Uncle explains, talking about Mother.

And in any case I have my village, a house, a bicycle, a station and I'm the sturgeon messenger. I reckon that's not bad for a boy of twelve.

XI

As far back as I can remember, there have always been sturgeons in the river. At least, they were here before me in any case. Because we used to live in a different village, not far from here, but with no sturgeons. Uncle was in Ferrara, working for the railway, then he got sent here, and promoted to stationmaster. Even back then he had an office, a little one, that he shared with other railwaymen. He worked in an office, he wasn't out mending the rails. He was in the freight office. I'm not sure exactly what that is but it sounds important. One day we went to visit him and he let me use the telephone. I'd never used one before. Uncle turned the crank and let me say hello to a colleague of his in another station. It was like a magic trick, hearing his voice. Uncle was magical too then, powerful and strong, with his moustache, but he cut that off later.

It was when we went to the city that I saw the caviar Lady for the first time. I saw her at home, in her shop, with the sign that says "Delicacies," where she makes the caviar. To be precise she makes the caviar in the backroom.

In the shop itself there was a prodigious display of sweets, herring, salt cod and salami that smelled so good it made you want to stay there forever. Cans of tuna, olives, peppers, salted anchovies, mushrooms preserved in oil, artichokes... Fine wines, flasks of Chianti, labels with names you couldn't make out, with gold medals, prizes from the Universal Exposition... And gold tins of caviar with bright red labels and the regal, imperial words: *Caviale del Po*. The tins were arranged all round the smoked sturgeon, which was ready to be sliced by the errand boy. That's where I saw him the first time, now I remember: he was younger, not much more than a boy, but tubby even then. He probably didn't sweat so much back then. Or perhaps it was covered by all the wonderful smells in the shop, that were swirled around by the ceiling fan. I don't remember anywhere more enticing than that shop, where the aromas, the tang of sweet and savory, spices, pepper, fish, hams... Ah, the ham: I reveled in that deep, intense, enveloping fragrance long before I actually tasted it. Like a game, each tin contained a different treat, an idea that formed in your head making your mouth water...

Uncle had his Sunday best on to visit the caviar Lady: his waistcoat, his pocket watch with the chain (something that became a familiar sight, once he was promoted to stationmaster), his bow tie and straw boater. He looked like a real man of fashion, a man of the world. And it filled me with pride to see Mother, who had had her hair done specially for the occasion, in the midst of all those scrumptious smells.

The backroom leads off from the shop.

"Come and see, Nellino," says Uncle. "Come and see where the food of the gods is made."

We go down the stairs and through a little door that leads to a room that is cold and white, like a hospital, with tiles that remind me of the butchers' shops full of flies where sometimes, but not often, Mother buys a piece of meat or a packet of tripe. But there are no flies here. In the corridor there's a piece of flypaper hanging up, but it must be new, because there are hardly any black marks, which are the flies. If I think of the flypaper in Nena's tavern which is all black... People joke about it, saying it's in mourning.

In the white room there are some women, all dressed in white, wearing hats like nurses' hats, cleaning up. There are instruments and boxes, but it looks more like a pharmacy than somewhere for the food of the gods. The only goddess is her, the caviar Lady, who greets us with a smile that is impossible to forget. As if we were her nearest and dearest. Uncle introduces us:

"My nephew Nellino."

And she holds out her hand, like adults do when they are introduced. I shake it. I look at the caviar Lady and the world around her seems different, kinder - that's how I would describe it today. She's smoking, but it's not noticeable, I don't even smell it. She speaks in a low voice and hands me a sweet, a barley sweet.

"For later," she says, giving me a wink.

She exchanges a few words with Uncle, but I can't make out what they're talking about. Books, maybe, but I'm not sure. Then she takes us through another door into a sort of house that has a large dining room with a few tables and chairs, where there are people sitting, reading and eating.

"Make yourselves at home," she says.

It's like a restaurant, but it's really a house. But there's a maid, who serves us broth with *passatelli*. Which is delicious despite the infernal smell of garlic that comes out of the tureen.

"Uncle, I think the cook must have put in too much garlic..."

Uncle laughs so hard he almost chokes. Then he gets his breath back. Mother looks at us both disapprovingly.

"It's truffle," says Uncle. "White truffle, pine forest truffle..."

After the broth they bring us meat: two slices of meatloaf that Uncle says is made of turkey, and fried pumpkin. What a feast. When pudding comes, which is sweet and creamy and tastes of lemon, I can't hold back any longer and blurt out:

"Mother, Uncle, what are we celebrating?"

"We're celebrating you coming to live with me," Uncle answers. Then he talks to the caviar Lady again, who won't hear of taking any money.

We leave a different way, not through the shop of delicacies. What a beautiful word that is. It has a wonderful sound.

I never got to go back there again.

XII

When the season's over life on the riverside gets a bit gloomy, but at least Nicola doesn't have to work that much and he gets to spend more time with us. The season lasts a few short months, and decides your whole year. From March, some years February, until May, or June, then it's all over, and the sturgeons are gone. If there are any still in the river they're not females and if they're females they've no eggs. In other words, no caviar, and even those for filleting are second rate, when they're late going back down to the sea.

The fishermen who have caught a lot of fish and got good prices can save up to get through winter. Some people take their money to the post office and others, and everyone knows who, keep it under their mattress. But that's just a figure of speech, because I've never seen a mattress in any of the houses on the riverside. They all sleep on straw pallets, maybe with a ticking cover, but inside it's straw, reeds, corn chaff, whatever people can get their hands on.

In the station apartment we sleep on mattresses, good ones, horsehair for summer and wool for winter. I don't like saying it, and sometimes I don't even notice it, but there is a difference between us, getting by okay but having to eke out our money, and the fishing families on the riverside, who are dirt poor. They have almost nothing because fishing is not like growing wheat that you can do every year.

As the Turk says: "Sturgeon fishing is like gambling in the casino. You can smell the money but in the end you lose the shirt off your back."

It takes luck, a whole lot of luck, to catch a sturgeon that can turn the year round and give you a chance to keep your head above water, pay off your debts and cover your expenses. And the year after? The people round here remember seasons when they didn't catch a single fish, and all the fishermen ended up so in debt that not even the air they breathed was their own any more.

Then some years, some of them made enough to buy a motorcycle or pay for drinks the whole summer. It's just a question of luck. Skill too, but above all luck. Just like in the casino, which among other things, was a word the Turk brought here, because no-one here had ever heard of it. At the end of the season the fishermen pay off their debts and take stock and there's never much stock. And now that there's not so many big spenders around we have to be careful not to catch too many sturgeons - we might not even be able to sell all the caviar, Mario's father says. He always sees the negative side of things. Mario's mother tells him to pray to Saint John the Baptist to catch the big females.

"The females I like are big here," he jokes, miming a big chest and making everyone laugh.

Mario's mother makes the sign of the cross and looks at Bechi and says, "May the good lord help you, poor child, look where you've ended up."

Bechi smiles, as always, because she has a lovely smile and it means she doesn't have to say anything.

Nicola asks what Saint John has to do with sturgeons,

"Isn't the Feast of Saint John the day for gathering walnuts?"

"Yes Nicola," I say because I always have to explain things. "But he's also the patron saint of the village, so he's the saint of the riverside and the Po."

The Turk smokes and hardly ever says anything. But he wants to reassure Mario's father because he knows he's worried:

"Rich folk always find money for caviar, don't you worry."

"If things carry on the way they are, there won't be any rich folk left," Mario's father replies.

So I tell Mario's father that Mussolini founded the empire so that everyone will be better off, even the fishermen on the riverside. For my trouble I get a kick in the backside, and I don't even know who it was. But one of these days I'm going to go to the Militia Corps and tell them that there are no good patriots on the riverside. The sturgeon season is over for this year, that's for sure, otherwise there would be no time for all this talk.

XIII

The cases that arrived in the station this morning all bear the words National Fish Stocking Program. Uncle looks at the rail car with a look that says he doesn't know whether to be mad, or telegraph the *Podestà*, or write to the rail superintendent, or make a formal complaint to the Duce in person, or be glad and find a solution. I too can see that having a cargo load of tench fry landing in your station with no prior warning is a big problem.

"Now I come to think of it," Uncle says after a while. "They told me they would be sending material to repopulate the drainage channels, to be distributed."

"Who to?"

"Someone has to sort it out. The party will know what to do. Nello, go and find the secretary and tell him to come here."

By the time I get to the barber's shop I'm out of breath and it's closing time, so I start shouting:

"Comrade Baffoni! Comrade Baffoni!"

"Who goes there?" comes a voice from the window.

"It's Nellino, the stationmaster's nephew."

"What do you want at this time of day?"

"There's a problem at the station."

"Call the Railway Militia Corps."

"No, the Militia Corps can't solve this problem, you need to come."

"Tell your uncle I'll finish my lunch and be right along."

"Comrade Secretary you have to come now, or they'll all die."

"All who? For the love of God, who?"

"Come, come quickly..."

I run back to the station, followed by Emilio Baffoni, the village's Fascist Party Secretary. He's the highest authority there is, though I'm not sure whether he's above or below the mayor.

"Scaramagli! Pompeo Scaramagli!" shouts Baffoni. "What's all this about then? Who's dying?"

"Take a look there."

"Well? It's a wagon-load of carboys."

"Ah, but you don't know what's inside them."

"Wine, vinegar, oil? Out with it Scaramagli. I was halfway through my lunch."

"Fish, Comrade Secretary, live tench fry for the National Fish Stocking Programme, to be distributed."

"And to whom, exactly? We've plenty of fish in the Po and the drainage channels."

"That's just it: I don't know. It's up to you to decide, but if we leave them out here in the sun they'll all die."

"Nellino!" barks Secretary Baffoni. "Go and call Donna Italia, the Secretary of the Rural Housewives Association. The women should decide."

"You mean your wife?"

"Yes, yes, my wife, but tell her to come in her capacity of secretary of the Rural Housewives Association."

I run back to the barber's house. When I get there I call:

"Donna Italia! Donna Italia!"

"What is it Nellino?"

"Your husband wants you at the station."

"What kind of mess has that idiot got himself into now?"

"Um, well, he told me you've to come in your capacity."

"In my capacity? Ah, you mean as Secretary of the Rural Housewives Association?"

"Yes, that's what he said."

"But what for? Has the Federal Secretary turned up?"

"No, no, it's not that. Come along and you'll see."

"What on earth have you done now you idiot?"

"Italia, Italia, can't you see I'm here as Party Secretary?"

"I'll give you secretary. You're good for nothing without me to sort out your problems."

"Take a look here."

"What is it?"

"Tench."

"Fine, let's roast them."

"No, they're too small."

"Then we'll fry them."

"But they're alive, they're for the National Fish Stocking Programme, from the Duce."

"And what are we supposed to do with them?"

"Distribute them to repopulate the drainage channels."

"Who to?"

"That's the question."

Donna Italia looks at Mother and says:

"You're a housewife, what would you do with these things?"

"I don't know," Mother says. "Maybe we should ask Don Antonio."

"Of course! That's who we need."

"Nellino, go and get the priest."

"But I'm hungry," I complain to Mother.

"Run and get him and then I'll get your lunch ready."

I run to get the priest and he hurries along to the station too, but only after I've told him they're all going to die. He's wearing his vestments and has everything he needs for the last rites, I know because I've seen him visiting the dead and dying before. Perhaps I could have explained it a bit better, but I can see that when I say they're all going to die everyone understands that it's a serious matter.

"Good day Don Antonio," they all greet him.

"Who needs to confess?"

"No, no-one. Look what's just arrived."

And they all start explaining the problem again. Don Antonio listens but he looks very cross about turning up in his vestments. I think that I'll probably have to talk about it in confession. After a long silence, he passes judgement:

"It's a question of fish. Ask the fishermen."

"Right you are," says Uncle. "It hadn't crossed my mind."

"I had thought of it, but down on the riverside we don't have a single party member," says Secretary Baffoni, clearly a little peeved.

"And I'll tell you why..."

We hear a voice from behind the wagon with the tench. And out comes Remo the signalman. He looks at Baffoni and raises his arm:

"*Saluto al Duce*!"

"*A noi*!"

We all stand to attention.

He gives a thin smile and says:

"We have no party members on the riverside because of that foreigner, the Turk."

Uncle shoots right back, almost too quickly:

"The Turk is a good Italian and if you contact him for this business I'm sure it will be the perfect opportunity to see to his membership..."

Remo looks at his boots. I try to hide but I can already hear the Secretary's voice:

"Nellino, go to the riverside and tell the Turk to come here right away."

I look at Mother, imploringly, but she just smiles back. I jump on my bike and race along the embankment.

"Nicola, Nicola!"

"Hey Nellino, want to come fishing?"

"You'll soon have more fish here than you know what to do with..."

"What?"

"Will you get your father?"

"He's in the woods cutting down poplars."

"It's urgent, get Bechi too."

When we get to the woods we can hear the Turk's axe chopping.

"Ah, the youth of Italy!" says the Turk when he sees us.

Whenever I see him I always think he's making fun of me a bit. Then he says to me:

"And to what do I owe the honor of a visit from you outside of sturgeon season?"

"We've got at least a million tench in the station."

"Like the homeland: eight million bayonets..."

"What did you say?"

"No, nothing, just a joke."

"You joke too much."

"And you not enough, for your age."

"You're not a member of the party."

"There's no need for it down here on the riverside."

"That's what you say," I reply, and I tell him the whole story. The Turk takes it all in, frowning.

"Come on," he says to Nicola and Bechi. "Run home both of you and get your black shirts on quick smart."

"But we don't have black shirts," Nicola objects.

"Bechi knows where they are..."

And she does. The Turk takes off his woodcutter's shirt and puts on a Fascist shirt too.

"You look good," I tell him.

"I know," he smiles back.

We get to the station looking like a military parade.

"*Saluto al Duce*!"

"*A noi*!"

"It has come to my attention that you are not a member of the party," Baffoni snaps, right away.

"In sturgeon season there's never time to come and enrol, and afterwards I am afraid I forgot," replies the Turk.

"See? You should have gone to him," Donna Italia scolds her husband. And she's right.

"Bring me my membership card, come down to the riverside one of these days and I'll get all the fishermen to join. Every last one of them, you have my word of honor."

"So, what are we going to do with all these tench?"

"We'll restock the drainage channels."

"But where? And how?"

"I'll take care of it."

"Nellino, would you please run to Nena and tell her that all the fishermen are to come here, with at least two flasks each, or three, or a demijohn if they have one."

"Flasks of wine?" I ask, not understanding.

"No, no, empty flasks."

"Empty?"

"Yes, empty."

I set off at once, even though I'm starving and it's way past lunch time now, because the Turk is the only one who said please. I'm not a kid any more. Or an errand boy. I get back on my bike and as I turn down towards the riverside I think that Remo will have to eat humble pie this time. Serves him right. Mother always buys from him what she can't find elsewhere, but he fawns over her in a way I don't like. By that evening all the fishermen had gone home with at least two flasks of tench fry to put in the drainage channels and ponds.

"Not in the Po," says the Turk. "The pike would make short work of them."

The Turk has joined the National Fascist Party, together with at least thirty fishermen. Uncle helped Baffoni write a letter to the Federal Secretary and the Duce to thank them for the National Fish Stocking Programme: feeding the new generations, Uncle calls it.

XIV

Nicola is my best friend. Actually he's more like a brother. Because we are both nobody's children, like the others used to say at school. I really miss him now I'm at middle school.

But he's my brother above all because he made me love the Po. I don't know whether it's sacred to the homeland like the Piave and the Tiber, but there's no doubt that it's the longest of them all. Seeing it from the riverside, it looks like the widest too. When it's in full spate and the fog comes down sometimes you can't even see over to the other side. When we talk about it I call it the Po, Nicola calls it the river. Of course he spends all his days there, and never goes anywhere else. And he believes, like pretty much all the fishermen do, that for good health you have to drink a glass of river water every morning. I, for one, am not convinced of it. On the days when the river is full to bursting, and cloudy and brown from the sand, I, for one, wouldn't dream of drinking it. But Nicola, who's the same age as me, does, and he's got great muscles.

I know that I'm fast on my bike, so fast I could be Bartali's teammate, or almost, but Nicola swims in the river and isn't scared of the currents, and the freezing cold water. Nicola swims like a fish. And he knows about fish, all the different kinds and how to catch them. And how to hunt with traps. And how to get the girls from the other houses on the riverside to show us their legs and panties.

"If I take my pecker out I'll get you all pregnant," he says to Rita and her sister Alba. They lift up their skirts and stick their tongues out, then they run away.

"I know where they are," says Nicola. "And they'll do anything with me..."

"Anything?" I gulp.

"Like this." And he unbuttons his pants and starts rubbing his pecker.

"That's all you ever think about!" I say disapprovingly, but I can feel my pecker is getting hard too.

"What are you two up to?"

It's Agnese, Rita and Alba's mother, who has seen us behind the nets.

"We're getting a rod to go and catch frogs," Nicola says right back.

And just as well, because I don't really know much about peckers. So we run to the drainage channel with rods and a bag for the frogs. Sometimes we catch them using our hands, but it's more fun with a rod. We cut the rods from the reed beds and tie a piece of string on one end. At the end there's a piece of red wool that the frogs bite on.

"Suck on that, whore," says Nicola, and he pulls up the string with the frog attached. We take it off and put it in the bag.

"Frogs sure are stupid," I say.

"Only good for one thing," says Nicola. "Like women."

"What?"

"Stupid, but good for screwing."
"Where did you hear that?"
"Mario's father said it."
"When?"
"The other day in the shed."
"He was there with Remo's wife, and she was sucking his pecker."
"What?"
"It's true you know."
"No it's not."
"It is, I'm telling you."
"Come off it, no-one *really* does those things."
"I'm telling you it's true, and he kept saying 'Suck on that, whore'."
"Nah, it's just you who says that, to the frogs."
"What do you know? You spend all your time in the station with your books. You haven't a clue what goes on in the real world."
"And you do? From spending all day on the river?"
"What's wrong with spending all day on the river?"
"Then what did Mario's father do?"
"He pulled up his trousers and said: 'Be off with you woman.' Then to me he said: 'You'll not be telling the Fascist now, will you? That's women for you son: stupid and only good for screwing.'"
"Who's the Fascist?"
"He meant Remo, the cuckold."
"What's a cuckold?"
"How old are you?"
"Thirteen, same as you."

"Ah, you're just a baby."

Well, that gets me really angry. I shout: "It's not true! Not all women are like that."

"Oh yes they are."

"My Mother isn't."

"Oh yes she is."

"Well, your father's a foreigner then."

"What's it to me?"

I land a punch on his nose, and he grabs hold of me and pushes me over. And we start grappling and rolling around.

"Bechi's not like that," I shout.

"Oh yes she is."

"If you lay a finger on her I'll break your legs."

"We'll see about that..."

"You can't, she's your cousin."

"Round here cousins can have kids you know."

I'm on the ground and I look up and see that Nicola is about to land me the kind of punch that knocks you out, but I've no breath left in me to fight back. So I turn round to see if there's anyone around I can ask for help...

"Hell's bells! You've left the bag open!"

"What bag?"

"The bag with the frogs, they're getting out."

Nicola lets go of me and runs after the frogs that are hopping everywhere.

"Come on, give me a hand!"

"Still think frogs are stupid?"

"Shut your trap and give me a hand."

We're not quick enough though, and half of the afternoon's catch is gone.

"Now what am I going to tell my father?"

"Tell him you were speaking ill of Bechi and God punished you. Or that you're an idiot. Up to you. What about me though? What am I going to say to Mother turning up at the station in this state?"

"Come back to my house and get yourself cleaned up. Oh, and y'know, Bechi doesn't really do those things."

"And neither does my mother."

"Yeah, I know."

Nicola smiles and spits on his hand: "Friends?"

I spit on my hand too and answer: "Yeah, friends."

We sing on the way home. In the copse we meet the Turk chopping down poplars for fire wood. Half for himself, half for the new doctor. That's the deal, but at least he'll keep warm through the winter.

"Ah Nicola. When you get home, tell Bechi to water the roses."

The roses are the only thing that makes the Turk's house different from the other huts on the riverside. All the others look like they were built in hard times. The Turk's is different. I mean, like the others, it's a hodgepodge of different kinds of bricks, and the wooden door is all swollen up with the damp and the roof shingles are moldering away in the fog, but it has a row of rose bushes at the front. Beautiful, proud red roses that seem to bloom all year round.

XV

"How you get them to flower like that?" Mother asks him, perhaps the only time that she goes to the riverside to see Bechi, to take her something, I can't remember what it was.

"Because it's my job," smiles the Turk.

"But aren't you a fisherman?"

Just like Uncle, with the Turk Mother uses the "lei" form of address, not "voi" like a good Fascist.

"In another life I was a gardener."

"Abroad," I add, proud that I know something about his life.

"Yes, when I was young I took care of the roses in the garden of the summer residence of the Italian Ambassador in Istanbul, in Turkey."

"And then what?" asks Mother, almost flirtatiously.

"Then there was the war with the Turks and the Italians had to leave."

"But you don't look that old. When was the war with Turks?"

"Mother, the Italian-Turkish war in Libya, where Uncle got his medal."

"The war in Libya? What's that got to do with the Turks?"

Perhaps Nicola was right, women are stupid. Not all of them

of course - not Bechi, not the school teacher, it was her who taught me these things - but Mother yes. At least this morning.

"What a pity," says Mother, looking at the roses. "You must have been sad to leave. But you were lucky, you know. I've heard certain things about the Turks. Was your wife Turkish too?"

The Turk is about to lose his patience. And I can understand him. But Mother keeps on, greedy for more tidbits. Me and Bechi listen in too. Nicola whistles, he must have heard it all before. He always pretends to know everything anyway.

"No, no, Lukina was Russian."

His voice sounds choked when he says the word Lukina. And his expression, normally so stern, gets softer. Sometimes one word is all it takes to change a person.

"Russian?" Mother says, taken aback. "But how come, if you don't mind telling me?"

"Because when I left Turkey I went to Russia."

"Don't tell me you were a secret agent?"

Mother is getting more and more stupid. I've never seen anything like it.

The Turk bursts out laughing: "No, no, nothing like that."

"Were you a political agitator like Nellino's poor father, then?"

The Turk gets all serious:

"I've always kept right out of politics. My life has been all work."

"Oh I'm sorry, I didn't mean to offend you."

"No offence taken. All I did was go to Astrakhan, with another gardener from the embassy. He was Russian. He told me there was plenty of work there so I went with him."

"And did you find work?"

"Oh yes, there was lots of work. We caught sturgeon that make the Po ones look like anchovies..."

"Sturgeon?"

"Oh yes, on the Caspian Sea, the biggest sturgeon in the world."

"So how did you end up here?"

"There was a war on in Europe, but in Russia there was a revolution too. It wasn't easy being an Italian far from home."

"You're *Italian*?"

"Of course. I'm from Ca' Badessa. My poor folks, may God rest their souls..."

Unbelievably, the Turk makes the sign of the cross, and even Nicola stops whistling at that.

"My poor mother and father were from there. They sent me into service with a family that became the Ambassador's family."

See how Mother does it? She pretends to be stupid but she draws the whole story out of the Turk.

"And what about the roses? How did you become a gardener?"

"I don't know what to call it: a gift, a chance thing? The first time I saw a rose, we looked each other in the eye and came to an understanding."

"You're quite the poet..."

"No, not me. I'm just a fisherman."

The Turk is back to his normal self now.

"You have to excuse me, I must be getting back to work."

"Do forgive me," says Mother, who has gone all serious now too.

Nicola goes after his father and Bechi says:

"Thank you for coming."

"Please think nothing of it."
"Goodbye."
"Goodbye."

I wonder why it is that no-one round here uses the proper "voi" form of address. When I ask Mother where Ca' Badessa is, she looks at me, thinks for a bit and answers: "I'm not sure. Somewhere along the Po I think."

Of course that's what you think. You think everything's along the Po somewhere. That's what I reckon, but I keep my mouth shut.

It's summer, and we've declared war on Russia. Victory should be imminent. At least that's what they said at the cinema in the village. And I hope it's true, because if people get word that Nicola's mother was Russian they'll start calling him a traitor too, like they do to me, because of my father. As if anyone can be blamed for the parents they get landed with. Especially because I know next to nothing about my father. I don't even have his surname, which was Costa. When I repeat it in my head – Costa, Costa, Costa – it makes me clench my fists and think it *cost* him too much to give me his name. He's not even on my birth certificate.

"He did it for you," Mother once told me. "He was a wanted man, and they would have been after you too." I believed this story for as long as you believe in Saint Nicholas or the Befana bringing gifts at Epiphany. Then one day you see your mother wrapping up the gifts from the saint and you realise it was all just a lie. My moment of truth came when I went to school: Romeo's surname is Costa but no-one has ever come looking for him.

The truth is that my father didn't take care of me, or

Mother. He didn't even marry her. And when he got killed Mother found out in secret from old friends. She didn't even know where her Menandro Costa was. Yes, my father had the name of a Greek comedy writer, that's what Mother always tells me. Then she always says:

"Do you know what a comedy writer is?"

"Of course," I answer patiently. "Someone who writes comedies."

But it's more a tragedy than a comedy, I think, to know your father was in Spain shooting at priests and crucifixes, when there were brave Italian soldiers volunteering to free Spain from the Bolsheviks.

I was old enough to see the Fascists march to victory. Mother and Uncle didn't even know where my father was. By then Uncle had been living with us for ages. Or rather, we had been living with him.

"At least this way I don't have to pay the bachelor tax," he said, laughing.

I found out that my father was dead because one day Mother came home crying. And for two days all she did was cry. Uncle scolded her and told her she was being stupid.

"What has that man ever done for you? Up and left you with this tinker. Stop crying and get on with your life." The tinker is me. And sometimes I think that maybe Mother was wrong. Maybe my father is someone else altogether. Maybe one day I'll wake up and he'll come for me. Riding a white stallion, who knows. And if I dream about it I'll tell Nicola and he'll catch a sturgeon for us. Oh Mother, why did you have to go and fall in love with a traitor, of all people?

XVI

I've always thought Bechi is beautiful. At least ever since the day she cleaned our kitchen floor. Now that she's grown a bit, and her chest has grown too, all the men have noticed and the Turk went to the tavern to have words with the riverside men:

"I've no daughters of my own, so Bechi is like a daughter to me. If anyone round here gets any strange ideas I'm telling you to take a dip in the river to cool off, because if anyone lays so much as a finger on her..."

And he mimes cutting his throat.

Some of them swallowed to see if their Adam's apples were still in place. Nena's eyes were shining, Nicola says. Everyone heard her because she really raised her voice and said,

"Hear hear! If only my father had spoken up for me like that... God rest his soul."

"Only he never did," said Battista the eel man, giving her a slap on the backside.

"Go to hell Battista," Nena answered right back. She was in no mood for joking around.

Battista is known as the eel man because he always catches loads of eels, even when there's a full moon and they all seem to go into hiding. He always takes those black snakes of his to market. Sometimes we tag along to spy on him.

"What do you think about what your father said about Bechi?" I ask Nicola.

"Nothing," he answers. "Because afterwards he took me aside and gave me a father to son talk, know what I mean?"

"Nah."

"He told me that things change at my age and that having girls around can be a dangerous influence. And that if I lay a finger on my cousin he'll cut it off. And the other one."

"The other what?"

"The other finger," Nicola says, pointing down there. And he laughs.

I think it's really stupid the way he thinks it's so funny to talk about the thing in his pants all the time. "Shut up, stupid," I say. "Surely you'd never really touch Bechi?"

"Are you crazy?"

"No, just asking, that's all. We're friends, it's not like I'm going to cut off your pecker."

"But she's my cousin..."

"Exactly. She's not your sister."

"Yeah but for me she should be like Our Lady."

"Who told you that?"

"Don Antonio."

"The Virgin Mary! The Virgin Mary!"

We chant it to Bechi as we go into the Turk's house.

She's cleaning the house, as much as anyone can clean a shack on the riverside, and she tells us to stop it, to stop acting like little kids. Well, that has an effect right away. We stand to attention, backs straight, shoulders back.

"That's more like it," she says. And laughs.

She might not be the Virgin Mary, but things have changed round here since she came. She is so like the Turk, you can see that they're related. You always get the feeling that she's got a secret, that she's hiding something. But there's no use asking her because she just smiles and leaves you hanging. Talking to girls can be really difficult. She doesn't even do the tomboy things that all the other girls on the riverside do. With Rita, little Alba, Marta, Benedetta, we often go to collect sticks for kindling in the woods, or duck hunting even though it's banned, or drive hares out of their dens, catch fish in the ponds and grub around for corncob husks to smoke. But as Nicola says, they don't mind showing you their panties, they're hardly the Blessed Virgin. To hear him talking about girls you'd think he's Casanova in person.

Bechi is more like the city girls, but we never see any of those round here so I don't really know whether she's like them or not. I think she is though, because when I'm in Ferrara and I stake out the girls' entrance opposite the boarding school in the morning, they all look a bit like Bechi. Well, she's prettier, but they act the same way. But Bechi is dirt poor. She's not like other poor people, I mean she reads books and sometimes she even stops to listen to us when we talk, but she's still dirt poor.

I can understand, though, why Mother cares about her: Bechi is really special. The riverside people say that even the Turk's character has improved since his niece showed up. Of course if he were able to send Bechi and Nicola to school, they would be a really nice family. He says he doesn't have the money, but I heard the secretary of the Party saying that he'd offered to help them out so Nicola could go to school. Maybe I shouldn't be so nosey. But what can I do? Nicola's my best friend and Bechi's his cousin.

XVII

The summer of '41 is the summer for fish. Every morning at dawn Nicola and me go out on the water. Sometimes we go to the sandy areas of the riverbank, where we try to net perch. On other days we put out pots to catch barbel, chub and roach, that Nena buys off us. She pays us in wine, sugar and coffee. It takes pounds and pounds of roach to earn a paper twist of sugar.

The Turk is happy, and Mother too, about this sort of summer job we've got. Uncle hardly ever worries about how I spend my days. He has to run the station, and organise the freight wagons, and in his spare time he reads the newspapers. He always buys a lot of papers, more than anyone could need and more than a stationmaster could afford, but for him it's like stepping into another life. He puts on his metal-framed glasses which is the signal that he won't listen to another thing. All the newspaper readers in the village read *Il Resto del Carlino*. I think Uncle likes to give himself airs by reading *Il Corriere della Sera*. Added to that is *La Domenica del Corriere*, the Sunday paper, which comes with illustrations. For me Uncle buys *Il Corriere dei Piccoli*, and me and Nicola read that, and the comic *Il Vittorioso*, hidden in the reed beds on the riverside or in the coves where there are huts that get used for the summer evening get-togethers, for fishing, for making out. I think the Turk lets us do it because deep down he doesn't really believe that there's no point in getting an education. I think he's glad Nicola still reads. Or that he sounds more educated than a fisherman's son should, as Dr. Girardi once commented, disapprovingly - it was around the time he was driving around in the Isotta Fraschini.

Apart from fishing on the Po, we also go to the drainage channels to put nets across the outflows to see if we can get any carp or tench. The fishermen, the real ones who live on the riverside, don't even know where the drainage channels are. They never leave the riverside, except to climb to the top of the embankment. All they have ever seen in their lives is the river, from ground level or the embankment. So when we turn up with carp, that live in the Po too but are not easy to catch, everyone wonders how we did it. We don't say how, but where, in the drainage channels, which just makes them turn up their noses.

It's the bicycle that makes the difference. They have their boats for going up and down the river, but we have bicycles, so we have broader horizons. Eel fishing is our real obsession. We've heard people say that in some markets eels fetch almost as much as sturgeon. It's not true. Whenever we've caught them we've made good money, but not that much. But we like to believe it anyway. We follow Battista the eel man in the evening, when everyone is out on the banks or drinking wine in the tavern. He leaves his house with a bag over his shoulder and we follow from a distance, staying out of sight. There's always the risk in the dark of stepping into a boggy patch and getting stuck in the mud. Then there's the risk of him seeing us and getting mad. Or him playing a trick on us. But when he sees us he doesn't get angry. He just gives us the slip. And we never manage to work out where he goes. We inspect the whole area the next day looking for his tracks, but there's nothing. I reckon he catches his eels in the Po itself. Nicola says he must know a hidden meander in the river. But how can there be such a thing as a meander so hidden that we haven't come across it in our travels yet?

"Maybe we're not going far enough."

"Maybe you can only get there by boat."

"But if you have to go by boat why does he go out on foot?"

"To lose us he makes us walk round the woods then he goes back to the riverside to get his boat."

"Nah."

"Might be."

It just might be. So one night we follow him, and after we lose him we don't go fishing as usual, but backtrack. We count the boats and the eel man's is missing.

"See? I was right!" Nicola whispers triumphantly. "Get in the boat and we'll go after him."

"Your father will kill us if he finds out we've taken the launch..."

"He won't see us, he's drinking with the others."

"And if he comes out and sees the boat's gone?"

"Get away with you... I'm second in command anyway."

"Yeah but have you ever taken the boat out in the dark?"

"You're scared of the river! It's not my father, it's the river!"

Nicola starts teasing me and I'd like to show him what for but this time he's right. I am scared. Scared of the river at night, of witches in the dark, of drowning, or not finding my way home, or encountering one of those monsters that are half men, half fish and half snake that the fishermen talk about during their summer evening gatherings.

Nicola tries to reassure me:

"There's nothing out here at night. Just eels."

"Just eels," I repeat to myself.

But as we go gliding along silently on the river current I can sense that there are all sorts of things lurking just below the surface. I've never been out in a boat at night. I've hardly even been that many times in the daytime. There's a strange kind of light that looks like it's coming off the water. You know you're alive because of the mosquitoes. We used to rub diesel fuel on our skin to keep them away, but since there's no diesel to be had for love or money these days, out on the river you get eaten alive. I can hear the water lapping against the side of the boat, which Nicola is controlling with an oar.

"See? I was right!" he says.

But apart from the water swirling beneath us I can't see anything.

"Look over there, where it's lighter."

There's a gap in the reeds. When the bow of the boat slides into the inlet we can hear waterfowl paddling on the surface of the water. And little splashes made by fish jumping.

"Carp," says Nicola. "This is the right inlet for the eels."

"The splashes are too big," I say. "It's sturgeon if you ask me."

"There's no sturgeon around now, they've all gone back to the sea."

We try to get a feel for the layout of this long, narrow inlet that is invisible from the riverside, and just might be where the eel man comes to fish.

Nicola approaches the bank and we hesitantly feel around for somewhere to attach the rope with all the lines and hooks on it. It has to be a safe place where no-one'll see it, because if someone steals our hooks there'll be no fish for us tonight. A branch almost takes my eye out, but at last it's the kind of branch we need, sticking out from an old tree trunk that's half buried in the sand. We tie the rope to it and push it under the water so it won't show. Then we start to put down our hooks, using an oar to push across to the other side of the inlet. The long rope, with fifty lines hanging from it, sinks out of sight under the water. Attached to every piece of line is a hook, and on every hook there is a worm, that we picked out of a heap of manure. It's a lethal weapon. We get across to the other side and look for something to tie the other end of the rope to. We'll come back at dawn. Fingers crossed it's our lucky night.

It's hard work getting home, we have to row against the current and the Po has big muscles even in the summer. I can't sleep, and spend the night tossing and turning. I even hear the cargo trains passing through, something I don't usually notice. It's still dark when I go down onto the station platform and see the locomotive handlers and hear the trains puffing. The steam is boiling hot in the cool morning air.

"Where are you off to Nellino?" asks Remo the signalman, who is lending a hand with the load and the maneuvers.

"Fishing..."

"Sooner or later the good times will come to end for you too..."

"I put food on the table you know," I object, testily.

"Well, if you've anything going spare you know where I live," he says sarcastically.

I can feel my blood start to boil but it's getting late, and we can't run the risk of being stopped by the Turk, because then he won't let us take the boat out. I reach the riverside and wait, out of sight like Nicola said. When I hear a low whistle I make my way over to him. We head back down the river, downstream, with the dazzling light of the morning sun in our eyes. The entrance to the inlet is impossible to spot by day too. Nicola points it out: it's like a little corner of paradise in there, birds and colors flashing over water that is green and blue and crystal clear. The smell of the herbs that grow on the river bank is more pungent here, and the river mud gives off its earthy tang. We reach our branch and start pulling in the line. On the third hook we find our first eel, writhing, huge.

"Get the rag, and put it in the basket."

We have a wire creel to keep the eels in, to make sure they don't escape. At the tenth fish we feel like we're the apostles on the sea of Galilee in the story Don Antonio read to us. But this here is a real live miracle!

There are a few tench along with the eels too. There's enough for everyone, for at least a week. We head back like Greek heroes, like Roman legionaries, like...

"Has no-one ever told you not to go stealing from thieves?" It's Battista the eel man, and he's waiting for us on the riverside.

"The river don't belong to no-one," replies Nicola.

"Well, this bit belongs to me, lad."

"He's got a point," I say. After all we did track him like spies.

"I could have cut off all your hooks if I'd wanted to."

It was true.

"And I could have kept all the eels."

That was true too.

"So?" Nicola asks, grudgingly.

"So we go halfers, from now on. And you can fish for eels whenever you like."

"There are three of us, so it's a three way split," Nicola answers.

"Well, you're a sharp one aren't you?"

Battista is right, Nicola is sharp. It would never have occurred to me. We split the eels. We get five each, which isn't bad at all, and I head home with my share. I walk past Remo's signal box and jump over the rails holding a writhing serpent in my hand.

"This is for you."

He makes a face but accepts. After all it's wartime and we're all hungry, even Remo who always seems to have a bit of everything in store.

XVIII

"Here's what I don't get: the more we win the war, the less of everything there seems to be. Why is that, Mother?"

"Perhaps because we're sending everything we can to support our soldiers at the front..."

"Yes but if we're getting closer and closer to winning surely we must have conquered something? Greece for example. Uncle is there nothing coming for us from Greece?"

Uncle raises his eyes from his newspaper, takes off his glasses and stands up.

"Why don't you go and ask the barber?"

"Who? Comrade Baffoni?"

"Yes. Ask him why we've got nothing left, not even diesel to run the *Littorina* railcars. We only see military trains running now. Getting people from place to place is more and more difficult."

"What are you talking about Uncle?"

"Just the truth Nellino, just the truth, but we are not supposed to say these things. Go and ask Remo why he has real coffee and sugar and eggs on sale for the price of caviar... Go to your Fascist friends and ask them why their sons still haven't been sent to Russia. Then go to your friends on the riverside and see how many youngsters are left. I want to see just who's going to be around to work in the fields next year. And who'll be left for the sturgeon fishing."

"But Uncle, who needs sturgeon when there's a war on? Our country needs iron, tin, weapons, soldiers..."

"And boys in black shirts..." retorts Uncle.

"Pompeo!" Mother glares at him.

"Yes Pompeo, Pompeo, but look at the state we're in, and him, at his age still believing in the final push for victory..."

"You're not turning into a subversive like my father, are you Uncle?" I'm almost afraid to ask.

"If only I was! Then I'd go and put a bomb up the Duce's backside."

"Pompeo! That's quite enough!" Mother says decisively.

She looks at me, with a worried look, but then she smiles and says: "Uncle's tired."

"But he's offending our Country."

"He's just saying what everyone's thinking Nellino."

"But it's not true!" I yell. "We're winning the war, one final push is all it'll take. Our boys are fighting like heroes, in no time we'll be in Moscow and the war will be over. The Germans..."

"Ha! The Germans!"

"Pompeo! Hush now! Do you want him to report you?"

Report Uncle? It hadn't crossed my mind, because I'd always thought he was a good patriot. But maybe Mother is right, maybe I should report him. Perhaps my father was not the only one with subversive leanings. Now Uncle too. No, it's impossible, they aren't even related. He's Mother's brother...

"Nellino."

Uncle has gone all serious. I can tell by the way he says my name.

"I want to speak to you man to man, but I want to speak to a real man, not one of those puppets hell-bent on marching on without even seeing if there's a road under their boots..."

I listen. It's Uncle's tone of voice... I don't know, I don't really understand why, but I know I have to listen.

"You're a good boy, you work hard, you love your family. And there's no doubt you're a good Italian too, but..." Uncle pauses carefully. "But you need to open your eyes. You can't just believe everything they tell you."

"But what about Il Duce? And the homeland? And the empire?"

"Nellino. It was fine when it was all just a game, but life is getting harder and harder every day. No-one can get by on their salary these days. Even people who've got money are having a hard time getting what they need. The conscription age is getting lower and lower - boys are getting called up now and even people who've already served are being sent back to the front. This war is not going to finish tomorrow and they say the worst is yet to come."

"But how do you know these things Uncle?"

"I listen to the radio."

I listen to the radio too, but I've never heard this kind of talk.

"Uncle, surely you're not listening to Radio Londra? Don't tell me you're a Bolshevik too?"

"Listening to Radio Londra doesn't make you a Bolshevik," says Mother, with an authority I had never heard before.

I look at Uncle and I don't know what to say. I can't hardly believe my ears.

"But you're a party member," I protest. "You do the Roman salute and everything..."

"Of course I do Nellino, I hardly have a choice!"

"So you're just pretending?"

"No, it's not that. It's just that there some things it's a good idea to do."

"And some things you can think but not say," adds Mother. "Do you understand what I'm saying?"

"Yes Mother, yes Uncle."

But to tell the truth I'm thinking about going to Secretary Baffoni and telling him I'm surrounded by subversives. In the end I tell Nicola, who's really my only friend. Nicola says that telling tales is the worst sin of all.

"Worse than treason?"

"Telling tales is treason," Nicola replies.

"I meant betraying the homeland."

"It's the homeland that's betraying us, there isn't even any coal to be had these days."

"What do you need coal for with all the wood you've got down on the riverside?"

"Just saying. Anyway, you know what happens to telltales..."

And he draws his finger across his throat, just like the Turk did that night in the tavern when he warned everyone off Bechi.

"Phew! I thought for a minute you were going to say they went to hell," I say, to lighten the atmosphere.

"Yeah, well that too," Nicola answers, seriously.

"Did Don Antonio tell you that?"

"No, I just know."

So there it is. He just knows. I don't feel like I know anything anymore. I thought Uncle was a patriot, getting the trains running on time, but now he's behaving like a Bolshevik. And Mother's going along with it! I thought I would never be interested in girls, just like Uncle. But now I like Bechi, only I can't pluck up the courage to tell her. Or even look at her. So I decide to tell Nicola, all in one go: "IreallylikeBechi..."

"What?"

"IlikeBechi."

I take a deep breath.

"I can't understand you, slow down."

"I like Bechi."

"What? You lay a finger on her and you're a dead man."

I look at Nicola to see if he's going to do his dad's cut-throat finger, but he's deadly serious. He's glaring at me just like Uncle did before.

"What did you say?" I ask, amazed.

"Lay a finger on her and I'll kill you."

"Hey! Don't get your knickers in a twist! I know she's your cousin and all, but..."

"I said, lay a finger on her and I'll kill you."

"Wait a minute..."

Now it's dawning on me, and I take another deep breath.

"Now you listen to me. If *you* lay a finger on her *I'll* kill *you*."

"I'd never touch her," says Nicola. "Not before I marry her."

"You? Marry her? But you've only just turned thirteen!"

"I can wait."

Now it's my turn to laugh because it's one thing being all serious and in love, but he's just being stupid. And now suddenly I understand something else too. I was so devoted to the homeland that I couldn't see that some of the things Uncle was saying are actually true. Not all of it, maybe, but a bit of it. Because Secretary Baffoni's sons, and Remo's sons didn't get sent to Russia, but all of Mario's brothers are away. And not by choice. And Remo always greets me with a Fascist salute, but then he tries to touch Mother and I always see big banknotes coming out of her purse when he brings her eggs. If Uncle was not at least a little bit right, Remo would be sending those eggs to our men in Greece. Or maybe he would give them to the shop because when we go to buy food with our ration cards there's hardly ever anything left.

"You never know, maybe you will marry her one day," I say jokingly to Nicola.

"Of course I'm going to marry her," he replies, totally in earnest.

"You'll need to learn a trade then."

"I've already got a trade."

"No you haven't, that's your father's trade. You're just the..."

"I'm the second in command."

"Does the Turk give you a percentage then?"

"What's that got to do with it? We're family."

"See? You don't have a trade."

"Neither do you."

"I'm going to be a lawyer."

"I thought you were going to be a doctor?"

"Yes, alright, but whatever I do I'll be coming to pick Bechi up in my car..."

"I can't wait to see you trying to get down to the riverside in a car."

Nicola laughs heartily, and it makes me want to laugh too.

In the end we go back to his place, arm in arm, chanting: welikebechi, welikebechi...

Once we are within sight of the house of course we stop. I get on my bicycle and head back to the station, where I cross paths with Uncle.

"I'm sorry I was impertinent," I say.

"Don't worry about it, I know you're growing up."

And he hugs me. I don't remember him doing that before.

XIX

’42 is a sturgeon season to remember. Everything was crazy: the people and the fish. And the river. By the end of the winter it was really low. In February the great Po gets lower and lower day by day. The cold makes the water sparkle and when the morning sun burns off the fog little wisps of white linger on over the riverside. Standing by the boats in the morning it’s like when you can see your breath in the cold air: even the river seems to be making white puffs of breath. It’s a Sunday at the end of the winter, so I’m not at school but down on the riverside. I told Mother I was going to mass. But instead I’m here with Nicola and Bechi, watching the Turk staring out at the river.

“He had a dream last night,” says Nicola.

“Was it the white horse?”

“No, no, if only it had been,” he shakes his head. “He had a dream about the lady...”

“The caviar Lady?”

“Yup, her.”

“He told me she was walking through the trees on the riverside, pointing at an exact spot, in the distance.”

“So?”

"My old man says it's a sign."

"A sign of what?"

"He doesn't know, he's looking at the river to try and work it out."

For a while we stand there and watch him looking at the river.

Then he turns to us:

"Hello Adam, did they tell you about my dream?"

"Yes, we were just talking about it."

"But not the whole story."

"What whole story?"

"That when I woke up I went out and heard noises."

"Noises?"

"Yes. Fish, jumping in the river."

"But it's still winter," I object.

"Yes I know, but look over there."

And he points out a line of current in the middle of the river.

"See?"

"I see the water."

"Yes but underneath."

"Underneath what?"

"The river bed is almost ready. Maybe the sturgeons are on their way. Today is the Lord's Day, but tomorrow we can get started. The boat and nets are ready, right?"

Nicola and Bechi nod.

"I still think it's too early," I say; being the messenger boy I do have a bit of experience, after all, and I don't remember there ever being sturgeons in February.

"So they're teaching you to fish in school now, are they?" the Turk asks, lighting his pipe.

"That's tobacco!"

"Indeed it is, son, indeed it is."

"But where did you get it?"

"I was saving it for the start of the season."

The sweet, pungent smell of the Turk's smoke envelops the riverside, sneaks between the huts and mingles with the white clouds of the river's breath. I can't work out whether the Turk is joking or not.

"Come down tomorrow as soon as you get back from Ferrara," he says. "We might be needing to send a telegram."

He gives me a wink and gets into his boat. He pushes off and glides away on the current.

"I'm going to have a look."

"Wait! I'll come too," says Nicola.

"No, you'll stay at home because from tomorrow you'll have more than enough to do in the boat."

"See what he's like," says Nicola dejectedly.

"You never know what he's up to, he just ups and offs, comes and goes as he pleases, gives out orders. Tomorrow, sturgeons, huh!"

"Maybe it's a joke for Carnival," I venture.

"No way! He never jokes about fishing," interjects Bechi.

We both turn towards her, she's usually so quiet.

"You'll see," she says. "He'll be right about this. The Turk never makes mistakes." And she gives us a knowing smile, the kind of smile that makes you feel like a little kid again.

"We'll see," I reply.

"Now do you see why I can't go to school, not even the trade school?" says Nicola.

"If school started in the summer and finished now, then I could."

"No point letting it get you down" I say. "Are you still reading?"

"Hey, what's happened to you? You sound like a right know-it-all."

He's right, how come I'm sounding like a know-it-all? I don't know. I don't say anything. I should probably go home. I go back the next day, after school. And Bechi tells me that the Turk and Nicola are still out in the boat, but that there is a telegram to be sent.

"They got one?"

"They got four."

"Four?"

"One's a female that weighs at least fifty kilos. They've tied it up here in front of the house."

I turn round and see the ropes attached to one of the posts of the little jetty. I can see the fish stirring up the water.

"Does it have eggs?"

"It's full, otherwise why would I tell you to send the telegram?"

The low water levels, the lowest I've ever seen, have brought us luck, at least as much as dreams have, anyway.

XX

There's something different from the other years and I can't quite put my finger on it. Then the day after the errand boy gets here it comes to me: there are no other boats ready to go out. All the other boats are dry docked, waiting to be mended, waterproofed, cleaned. Some have just been left lying in front of the houses. There are no nets hanging out, ready for the start of the season. And it's not because it's early on. Fishermen are far-sighted folk, they know the season can start at any time and that you always have to be ready. No, what it is, is that there are no fishermen.

"I don't know, we'll have to see what we can do," the Turk says to the errand boy who has travelled up with great pomp and ceremony in first class. Not even the lady herself ever travelled in first class. He's fatter than ever, red-faced, with new glasses, a watch chain on show and a dark suit of good cloth. He has a ring on his left hand, a gold wedding band.

Mother whispers to me: "Well, look at that! I thought all our gold was supposed to go to the war effort."

"It is," I say.

"Did you get married?" she asks, never one to mind her own business.

"Yes," he answers.

"Well, congratulations!"

"But what about the gold for the war effort?" I ask.

"What are you talking about Nellino?"

"No, no, it's nothing," Uncle intervenes, inviting the errand boy up into our flat. He gives my arm a hard squeeze as he goes past.

Now along comes a skinny boy who might be around my age, with freckles, loads of obvious looking freckles, not like mine that you can hardly see any more. He gets out of third class. "Morning."

"Good morning," we all chorus.

"Aldo, my assistant," says the errand boy.

"I've brought him along so he can learn the trade."

So he can learn to sweat like a pig and make a zig zag mess of the fish, I think to myself. With his gold wedding ring the errand boy is different. Like Dr. Girardi with the Isotta Fraschini. I look at him, and see the Fascist Party badge in pride of place on his lapel. Uncle gets there before me:

"Have you joined the party?"

"Naturally. Our country needs us, and Mussolini, let me tell you, is the man who will lead us to victory."

Uncle says nothing.

"Just as well the season's started, because I'm over-run with orders," the errand boy tells the Turk.

"One freeze would soon put a stop to it," the Turk answers.

"Well, let's hope not, because I've orders coming in from all over the world. My caviar is in great demand."

"In wartime?" asks Mother.

"My dear lady, my customers don't care two hoots about the war. I even have Americans writing to me for my caviar."

"But aren't the Americans our enemies?" I ask.

"Well, those who want the caviar aren't exactly American," the errand boy shoots back. "They're cosmopolitans."

"What?"

"Don't you worry about it. It's not like we're selling arms to those scoundrels, just fish eggs," says the errand boy, pulling in his stomach and puffing out his chest.

I keep thinking that his collar button is going to pop off, but they must have sewn it on double tight.

"There won't be a lot of caviar this year," says the Turk.

"Why not? The season has got off to a great start. And early too."

"Yes I know, but there's no-one to fish this year..."

"Ah! So when there's work to be done everyone makes themselves scarce, eh?" says the errand boy, clearly vexed.

"What else have they got to do?"

"Go to war," answers the Turk.

"Almost all of the younger fishermen and the sons of the older ones have been sent to the front."

"For crying out loud!" says the errand boy, who obviously hasn't taken that into consideration. "Well, the ones that are here will just have to work harder, organise shifts."

"And who's going to look after the boats and keep the nets in good nick?"

"I don't know, but I need you to organise the fishing, because everyone wants our caviar, a great Italian product that is the envy of the world."

And as he says this he holds out a five hundred lire banknote to the Turk.

"To cover expenses."

Mother's eyes widen and she says: "The Lady will be happy there's such a demand for it."

"Haven't you heard?" the errand boy exclaims, startled.

"She's left the trade, I thought she would have told you," and he looks over at Bechi who shoots him a dirty look back.

"No, we didn't hear anything," says Mother.

But Uncle looks uninterested. You knew, didn't you Uncle, I think to myself, but decide to keep it under my hat. Man to man.

"I'm the owner of the shop now."

"Well, congratulations again," says Mother. "That's a move up for you."

The Turk doesn't seem to be listening either. So he knew too, I can see that now. I don't know how, I just do. It's like growing up all of a sudden. I can see that there's some kind of arrangement, something else going on, between Uncle and the Turk. I realise that although they're very different, they're in this together. It's the kind of friendship that goes beyond who you are, what you do. Like me and Nicola.

"There's the train," says Uncle. "We'd better get a move on."

The errand boy bids us goodbye and off he goes with the first case of caviar of the 1942 season, and Aldo, the errand boy's assistant, as he will be known from that day on. I accompany them to the platform. When I get back to the flat I can hear Uncle, the Turk and Mother having a heated discussion.

"A great Italian product that is the envy of the world..." The Turk imitates the errand boy's grating voice.

"It's anything but envy," he says, in a serious tone. "There's probably a shortage of caviar now that Russia's at war and no-one has time to fish. What with German soldiers and our own on their hands, they certainly won't have time to think about fish eggs..."

"And all those 'poor cosmopolitans' dying of hunger." Uncle mimics the errand boy again.

"It must be big business if he's going round handing out five hundred lire bills without even worrying who's watching," says Mother, who seems to have put her thinking cap on instead of making funny faces and asking stupid questions as usual. I stay stock still in the stairwell, flat against the wall behind the door. I even hold my breath so I can hear them better.

What the Turk's saying about Russia has really impressed me. I've always thought he was just a fisherman. A great fisherman, but nothing more. But to hear him speak like that you can tell he knows the ways of the world, things I never would have thought of. I console myself with the thought that I am just a boy. Uncle is speaking now, saying that if it is true that everyone wants our caviar it is an opportunity we cannot pass up, because it's been a hard winter for the families down on the riverside, and next year won't be any better.

"You're right: if there was a bit more money to go round there are a lot of things people could do with buying."

"Well, they wouldn't get much for their money at Remo's. It's daylight robbery!"

"I know. But without the black market we wouldn't have a hope of getting anything."

"Well, it's a pity Remo doesn't sell extra workers," says the Turk.

Uncle speaks up: "Maybe we could ask the priest."

"Don Antonio? Expecting a miracle now, are we?"

"What about Baffoni?"

"Great idea! He can send us some Fascist Youth and we can open a nursery..."

"There's no two ways about it. Without hands on deck there'll be no fishing this year..." It's true what they say, the gods send nuts to those who have no teeth. I reckon that a good season would see us a bit better off too. Maybe there would even be enough for a present or two for me. On the riverside only children and old people are left. And the women, of course. As that very thought comes to me I hear Mother saying: "The women will have to fish."

"No, they're just not strong enough."

"What do you mean they're not strong enough? Those women work all day long, cleaning their houses, looking after their vegetable patches, tending to their children, gathering wood, doing all that washing."

I can tell the Turk is mulling this over, because he's not saying anything.

"But they'll still have to do the housekeeping and look after their children."

"If they go out fishing their children will be looked after," replies Mother. "The little ones can be looked after by their older brothers and sisters, it's the only thing not in short supply on the riverside - brothers and sisters of all ages."

"True, but they'll have to learn to fish."

"You can teach them," says Mother.

"But I have to fish..."

"All the boats will give you a percentage," says Uncle.

"And what about the upkeep of the boats..."

"They'll make up for that too."

The Turk remains puzzled: "We'll have to go round all the houses explaining it."

"No, all we need to do is tell Don Antonio."

"Who won't agree."

"Who will agree if we explain it all to him," says Mother, with a smile that disarms the Turk.

I mean, I can't see her, but I know her smiles and how they just melt away the tension. Well done Mother, I think to myself. And I go into the flat because all squashed up behind the door in the cold is not exactly a good place to be.

"Ah there you are, where did you get to?"

"I was looking at the shunter."

"But it's not doing anything, there's no coal."

"That's why I was there, to get a good look at it."

Uncle looks me over, unconvinced, I know he's smelled a rat.

"You're to go and get Don Antonio," says Mother.

"What am I to say?"

"Ask him to please come to the station."

"What for?"

"No reason, but it's urgent."

"Why don't you go to the church then? You'll get there faster," I say to Mother.

"At this time of day? On foot? It'll only take you a minute on your bicycle, and if the priest takes his bicycle he'll be here in no time."

He's hardly going to come running after that day with the tench, I think.

So I say: "Why don't you come with me Mother?"

"Me?"

"Yes, on the crossbar."

"Alright then."

So I go into the village with Mother balancing on the crossbar of my bicycle. Since she's had the idea of the women fishing she's like a different person. Joan of Arc, I would say.

Mother convinces Don Antonio, who goes to speak with the Turk to work out the details. The Turk not only spells it all out to him, but even tells him he has five hundred lire for expenses.

"The fool," says Nicola when he's telling me about it.

"What did the priest say?" I ask.

"That my father should not get any strange ideas about women whose husbands are away at war, that the fishing is to help families in need and that part of it has to be donated to the church."

"Well, there's a surprise!"

"Then my father said that we need to arrange a meeting at Nena's as soon as possible. Don Antonio burst out laughing and said that the Turk had strange ideas about the women on the riverside if he thought any of them would set foot in the tavern. And he warned him about having a meeting with that many people, because there might be trouble, times being what they are."

I am starting to understand that these are strange times we're living in. I've been thinking for a while now that the final victory is not going to be that imminent after all.

Nicola continues: "So my father asks Don Antonio how they could organise it and he says to come to church on Sunday morning, and he'll make sure that all the women, or almost all of them, are there, after mass. My father wanted the men there too, but Don Antonio told him that that was his problem. He said that if my father could get them to come to the tavern he could surely get them to come to church. He even got in a parting shot, about most of the men already going to church. Apart from my father that is."

XXI

It wasn't easy to begin with because women together cackle more than a flock of geese. And the idea of going fishing wasn't everyone's cup of tea. Some of them even crossed themselves, saying it was men's work. Then Mother went into action, with her calm smile. First of all she explained it in words that everyone understood. Then she answered their questions, and told them that Don Antonio was all for it. In the end, down on the riverside, she even got involved in organising them. Because it's one thing to take decisions, another to get the work done. I have to say that Mother turned out to be really good at it. She managed to get Donna Italia and the Rural Housewives involved too. She didn't explain that this year the caviar is more important than other years, that it's worth more, and that was something she didn't really spell out to the women on the riverside either. She just told them that in wartime everyone has to do their bit and the Po is full of fish. Donna Italia said she agreed and would even write to the Federal Secretary to recommend Mother for a commendation.

The riverside women know that fishing is their bread and butter. But they also know that sturgeon fishing is a lottery. It's like gambling in a casino, as everyone round here now says after the Turk told us what the word meant. But betting together means a bigger chance of hitting the jackpot.

So while some are mending the nets and cleaning up the boats that looked like they were just going to rot away for the rest of the war, the Turk prepares two wooden rods to dredge the riverbed. It's never been done so carefully, dragging two great boulders tied to ropes up and down the river. First one side, then the other. Broadening out a few metres every time. All sorts of mess come up from the riverbed, and where there are bigger tree trunks and sunken wrecks they put out buoys with flags, attached to big stones, to signal that there is something that could damage the nets.

The question of the music is taken very seriously after the Turk talks to Don Antonio. The men at war could have imagined anything but this happening in their absence: forty sturgeon boats waiting in line for their turn and passing along like a dance, one day upstream of the bridge, the next day downstream. And often in the middle boat stands Don Antonio himself, singing hymns but also opera arias, accompanied by a pedal harmonium. He is a sight to see: playing, inspired, in the middle of the deck, with Paride the sacristan in the stern trying to keep the boat balanced with one long oar. Don Antonio reminds me of Captain Ahab in Moby Dick that I have just finished reading. Only he, the priest, uses music and his voice to call up the sturgeons in the Po. The women in the launches with the nets follow the priest's lead and the whole river echoes like one huge theatre. The men, the fishermen, those who have always been here, who are left here, the old men, find themselves in the midst of it all and can do no more than shake their heads. There's never been anything like this before. But it's working. Everyone's fishing and it's the biggest turnout that the riverside has ever known. Every so often someone asks Don Antonio to sing one of the popular songs or a patriotic anthem, a party anthem, but he replies quite seriously saying that sturgeons are not fish for two-bit marches and café orchestras. Sturgeons deserve important music, holy music, written by greats for greats. Tavern ditties and parade songs were fine for catching roach.

On the banks all the children, those who are not in school, watch the boats waltz up and down the river.

"You could write an opera about this," says Mother, in awe of the perfect organisation of the fisher-women who have me running to telegraph the errand boy once or even twice a week. Then they need to sell the meat too, and more often than not that gets sent to Milan. Remo often buys it too, now he's got well-off families to supply on the black market. Donna Italia gets her share, so the Fascists, at least the local ones, are taken care of.

XXII

It doesn't go down at all well with Uncle that the errand boy and Aldo have started to come to the station in a brand-new Lancia Ardea. It has to be said that there are fewer and fewer trains to and from Ferrara these days and it looks like things will get worse because there's no coal for the locomotives or fuel for the Littorina railcars.

"In theory petrol for cars is rationed too," comments Uncle when he sees the Lancia Ardea.

But the errand boy gets away with it by keeping his party badge on show, and probably greasing the right people's palms. I have to study because I've got my exams this year. But even a distracted student can tell that it really gets Uncle's goat to hear the sound of that car. Uncle loves his station and his trains, I can see that now. The errand boy is always complaining to the Turk that there's not enough caviar.

"There aren't any more sturgeons in the Po," the Turk replies. "And we have to be careful not to kill all the females or there won't be any next year..."

"Don't worry about the future, worry about the present," says the errand boy.

"I'm behind on my orders. Everyone wants it, and they want it from us."

"Yes but you're getting all we've got."

"You could always do seconds," the Turk says one day, when he's had enough.

"What do you mean?"

"On the Caspian Sea they have different types of caviar."

"Really?"

"The highest quality of all is what they call *Beluga*."

"Yes, yes, I know, like ours..."

"Then there are the less valuable types, *Sevruga* and *Osetra*..."

"Yes, I know all this too, but we don't have those kinds of sturgeon."

"But we do have other kinds."

All of a sudden the errand boy looks interested.

"What do you mean, other kinds?"

"You, and the Lady before you, have never been interested in the fish, just the roe. I know the Lady wanted Beluga sturgeon or common sturgeon, which are bigger but more difficult to catch..."

"Get to the point man…"

"In the Po we get a lot of Cobice sturgeon that are much smaller - maximum twenty, twenty-five kilos. The eggs are smaller and darker and therefore less valuable."

"Maybe they're not even that good," the errand boy cuts him off.

"They are excellent," the Turk replies earnestly.

"And how would you know?"

The Turk pulls his mother of pearl teaspoon out of his pocket.

"You, you, you..." stutters the errand boy.

"Let's just say I have a cosmopolitan past," the Turk smiles.

The errand boy is rooted to the spot. He rallies, tries to look nonchalant and says:

"So that's why the Lady placed such trust in you. Because you're not just a fisherman."

"True. I am not a fisherman."

"Just what are you then?"

"A gardener," says the Turk, laughing, showing teeth that are as white as ivory, as white as the mother of pearl spoon.

I observe the scene and I feel proud to be Nicola's friend, and proud that the Turk is his father.

"We'll call it Venetian caviar," the errand boy enthuses.

"Why? We're not in Venice."

"I know, I know, but it sounds good."

"Call it Ferrara caviar."

"No, I'll call it Italian caviar."

"I don't know if you'll sell much to the Americans."

"Quiet, for heaven's sake, the boy is listening."

"You can trust Nellino."

The errand boy looks at me. He catches his breath and says: "We might not manage to sell it to the Americans, but with the aristocrats in Spain, Switzerland and Germany, and the Fascist big wigs, I think it might just work."

"You can call it what you like."

"When can I try it?"

"As soon as we catch some Cobice I'll let you know. But if we start catching these smaller fish you might need to come up from Ferrara every day."

"I'd come twice a day if I had to."

One look behind those glasses and you can see he's counting money in his head thinking about the Cobice sturgeons, the caviar of Venice, Ferrara, Italy or whatever he's going to call it. He's probably also thinking that if he comes every day he'll save money on telegrams. Or maybe not, maybe I'm just too hard on people. In the space of a few months I've completely changed: I used to believe in everything – Mother, the homeland, the empire – and now I don't trust anyone. I don't remember exactly when it happened, but it's happened alright.

I hear Uncle opening a bottle of Lambrusco, which is only for special occasions, and proposing a toast to the new caviar. I get a glass too, along with the errand boy, Aldo, the Turk, Uncle and Mother. As soon as the Lancia Ardea is out of sight, Mother says to the Turk:

"We should set up our own caviar factory. Here, in the village. So the women who fish could keep working, once the war is finished."

"But we don't have caviar all year round."

"I know. But it could be like the sugar plant: four months of work would be enough to see you through the rest of the year. Especially seeing as they are different seasons: the women could do four months in the sugar plant and the other four in the caviar factory."

"Caviar is for the gentry," the Turk reminds her. "You can't make it in just any old factory."

"I know, but if the errand boy manages it..."

"He might not exactly be charming, but he worked with the Lady for years. He knows the trade and we don't."

"Not even you?" asks Uncle who must have overdone it with the Lambrusco, seeing as he uses the familiar "*tu*" form of address with the Turk.

"Not even I know how to make caviar, at least not like the rich folks want it."

"Then we'll send someone to learn how to do it."

"We could take on that boy, Aldo..."

"One step at a time," the Turk is serious.

"This is no ordinary year, and it will help everyone pull through these hard times, and let people buy stuff on the black market. But we can't expect the other years to be like this."

"Why not?" asks Uncle.

"Because sooner or later the fish will run out."

"Nonsense! There have always been sturgeon in the Po, and there always will be."

"That's not the way it works. If only a few females lay eggs this year, it means that in a few years' time there will be fewer fish, and so on and until there are none at all."

"What a pessimist!" says Mother. "I'm sure we'll be able to change your mind."

"The fish are here to serve progress!" shouts Uncle, glass in hand. "Long live caviar! Long live progress!"

The Turk shakes his head, but says no more. He can see that Mother and Uncle like the idea of the factory and don't want to give up on this new dream. I like the idea of the factory too. And progress. Also because at the end of the season Uncle tells me to work hard for the third grade exams, and warns me that I'll have to study even harder next year.

XXIII

The final victory continues to be delayed. It still gets announced from time to time, but I don't really believe in it any more. Nicola sometimes comes round in the late afternoon, bringing clumps of poplar mushrooms for Mother. She invites him to dinner, but he excuses himself and says he has to go. So I come down from my cubbyhole, the space Uncle has set up for me to study in, in a dormer window in the station gable, and run to see Nicola.

"Still good at finding mushrooms, eh?"

"Yes, but it's no fun any more, now you're not here..."

"You know I'm at school in Ferrara."

"You were last year too."

"Yeah, but this year they're making us work twice as hard, so I end up spending half the day on the train, half at school, and the other half studying."

Nicola looks at me puzzled: "Just how many halves have you got in a day?"

"One more than other people," I reply, laughing.

"I heard you got glasses," Nicola says.

"Who told you?"

"Not telling."

"It was Bechi, wasn't it?"

"Nah, no way..."

"Come on, I know it was her..."

"You're the one who came down to the riverside on Sunday morning looking all brainy with your glasses on..."

"No, it wasn't that. I promised I'd read her some poems..."

"You think Bechi can't read?"

"You're jealous!"

"She kissed me, you know."

"Who, Bechi? No way."

"It's true you know. She kissed me right here."

And he points to his mouth, all defiant.

"Liar!"

"What about you then? Coming to my house in secret, with glasses on..."

"What's that got to do with anything? Anyway she never kissed you."

"Oh yes she did."

"If she had, your father would've beaten the living daylights out of you."

"I'm hardly going to tell him."

"She'll tell him."

"No she won't. She likes it."

"I'll tell him them."

"Hah! You lot are all the same. Going to school to learn how to snitch on people."

Now Nicola's really asked for it, and I land a right hook on his nose. This time I'm going to break it. But the scoundrel has seen me coming and dodges to the side leaving me outstretched, almost falling on the tracks.

"See what an idiot you are? You'd fall under a train, for the sake of a girl."

"There aren't any trains."

"Anyway I'd do it for Bechi, not just any girl."

"What are you two up to out there?" Mother appears at the window.

"Nothing."

"I've got to go now. In the evening I give Don Antonio a hand" says Nicola.

"The priest?"

"Yes, I help him out and he's teaching me to sing."

"Since when have you liked music?"

"It's work, not pleasure."

"You want to be a singer?" I look at him, incredulous.

"No, no. It's for the fishing."

Of course. I was completely forgetting the whole thing about music for fishing. After just two months of school, everything out here by the river seems like another world. You can see right away that we're not as close as we used to be. Nicola is wearing trousers of his father's that swamp him, and a sweater that is all matted from being out on the river. That alone says he's from the riverside. On top of that, a dingy colored jacket and a beret. He's never looked more like the Turk's son. Okay, so I wear Uncle's jacket and trousers to school, but at least Mother has taken them up for me. And today I've got a very smart white sweater Mother knitted for me, and a neck scarf. And I've started smoking, everybody knows anyway. Uncle even gives me a good cigarette every now and again.

"I've got to go."

"Bye then. If I manage I'll come down on Sunday, maybe we can go fishing."

"There are pike so big they're eating the mallards."

"We should make them eat Germans, not the poor ducks," Uncle comes towards us, smoking, with a smile.

"How's your father?" he asks Nicola.

"Fine, thank you. We're all grand."

"Tell him I was asking after him."

"I will do."

"What are you saying Uncle? Talking ill of our allies?"

"Piffle! Fine allies they are Nello! Do you know the Germans are using the railway without even asking now?"

"But there aren't any Germans here. I mean there aren't many."

"Enough of them to behave like they own the place. See this?"

And he shows me a sheet of paper, but it's in German so I can't understand what's written on it. It has the insignia of the Reich, that much I can see.

"I don't understand."

"I do. And it says that their trains have priority. On my railway. If a German convoy comes along I have to stop my train and make all the passengers wait - everyone going to work, you going to school. All because of this damned war."

"You want to watch what you're saying." Remo's voice comes from the shed beside the freight office.

"Just idle talk, Remo..."

"We were talking about what our enemies are saying," I butt in.

"Don't worry, I didn't hear a thing. But just be careful, because other people might. And you know the Germans are our allies. Right?"

"Absolutely," replies Uncle.

"By the by, did you know that in Germany they make the most delicious butter? Wait here a minute."

Remo hops across the tracks, and disappears behind his house, or rather behind the signal box, where he keeps his ice-box, and comes out with a paper package that you can just tell contains something delicious.

"This is German butter. A gift for your sister," he says, handing the package to Uncle.

"As soon as this war is over you'll see things will turn out just fine for all of us. Evening Pompeo, evening Nellino, and regards to your mother."

XXIV

The war is not going well. Even the news reels from the front are starting to admit that it won't be over tomorrow. Or the day after. In the village the Fascists are still organising their Saturday youth rallies and broadcasting the Duce's speeches on the radio. But everyone is tired.

"If there have to be wars, they should be short," Uncle pronounces.

In Ferrara too, where I now spend more time than at home because of school, things are not much cheerier. Also because it's winter and there's very little wood or coal and even though our school is for the future executives of the country and the regime, we are hardly ever allowed to have the stove on. It was Mr. Baratti, the Greek and Latin teacher, who said the thing about future executives, at the beginning of the school year. It took me a while to understand it wasn't anything to do with executing people. Executives are some kind of leaders.

Mr. Baratti often speaks in Greek and Latin. And his Italian is different too. Different from the Italian we speak at home, and hear on the radio or in the cinema. He is always quoting one writer or another - Manzoni, Dante, Leopardi, Foscolo,

Virgil, Julius Caesar, Cicero, Xenophon, Menander... My father's name was Menandro.

One day something bad happens. At the beginning of the year a new boy joined our class. He was from Milan and his name was Umberto Salvi. Milan was bombed at the end of October, no-one knows how, given all our powerful ground to air defence forces and the formidable Italian bombers, and the even faster, more formidable bombers of our German allies. Basically no-one knows how they managed it, but British planes bombed Milan. Just a few bombs, they said on the radio, cruelly dropped on unarmed civilians. We will not back down.

But Salvi's parents obviously got the wind up and sent him to his uncle and aunt in Ferrara. That was how he wound up in fourth grade at the beginning of November. He's not the most likeable of boys. He hardly ever speaks, and when he does he's a real smart alec. He keeps himself to himself, and he's not the only one. I tried making friends with him but you could see he wasn't interested. Then it turns out he has something to hide.

One day after school he is approached by three men. He tries to get away, but they stop him and bundle him into a black car, I think a Fiat, a model I've never seen before. In the village it's not like we get many cars, not like in Ferrara anyway. None of us can understand what's going on. We start talking about it but then I have to run to the station to catch the train. I tell Uncle about it and he looks me in the eye and says:

"These are dark times. Be careful of the company you keep in the city."

"But if I can't even see my school friends who's left?" I object.

"Just you be careful. And don't tell your Mother."
"Why not?"
"We don't want to go frightening her for nothing, do we?"
The next day, fortunately, the mystery is solved. A Militia officer in uniform, a man in plain clothes I have never seen before, and the headmaster, all come into the classroom.
"Doesn't Mr. Martani think he's the cat's whiskers now? My father says he's only headmaster cause of his black shirt," whispers Cavicchi, who's from Ferrara and always knows everything about everybody.
It's Mr. Baratti's lesson. The Militia officer gives us a short talk on race and what the laws have to say on the matter. He tells us that it is the duty of every good Italian and every young Fascist to report to their teachers and superiors anything that might seem against the law, any suspicious person or behaviour. It can all contribute to the final victory.
The man in plain clothes asks us how well we knew our classmate Salvi. Then the headmaster says we've nothing to worry about, that Salvi is Jewish and did not respect the laws that forbid Jews from attending Italian schools. And he did this in the typical underhand fashion that Jews have: under a false identity. Lucky for us the political police, ever ready and alert, represented by the comrade in plain clothes, expose Jewish infiltrators. They arrested Salvi, whose real name is actually Rimini. We all laughed when we heard what Salvi's real name was. If you have the same name as a city you can hardly be a normal person, being Jewish is the least that can happen, I think to myself.
"No one else here has anything to fear," the headmaster concludes, looking at Mr. Baratti. "We have ascertained the

ethnic origin and race of every student. And in any case this is one of the most respected schools in the Kingdom. We cannot shirk our duties to our country. Especially now that our finest young men are fighting on the front line to give us the chance to study. Isn't that so, Mr. Baratti?"

Baratti is looking at his feet. The formidable Baratti himself, who only has to lift his chin to cause a deathly silence to fall in any classroom. Baratti raises his eyes to the headmaster and mutters:

"He was just a boy, and a promising one at that."

"But he broke the law: he's Jewish. And there's nothing to stop him studying at home."

At that, Baratti regains his air of authority, looks the headmaster right in the eye and says:

"Tìs d'estì gnésios, tìs d'estì nòthos, pròs tòn theòn genòmenos anthròpos?"

"There's no need to quote Aristophanes at me now Mr. Baratti."

"It's Menander," Baratti corrects him.

The policeman in the coat raises his right arm:

"*Saluto al Duce*!"

"*A noi*!" we all chorus back with our arms up.

Mr. Baratti only puts his arm halfway up. Everyone files out, Baratti too, the hour is over. Albertini, who knows shorthand, has written down the phrase and passes it round. That evening I read it to Uncle who translates it right off, before I can even get my dictionary out:

"Who is a nobleman and who is a bastard, if in the name of the gods he is born a man?"

I don't say anything because I'm starting to understand.

And Uncle doesn't say anything because he doesn't feel much like talking these days.

The next day we have a supply teacher, Mrs. Boldini.

"Mr. Baratti has been taken ill," says the headmaster. "He will not be returning to school this year."

Or the year after. The radio, not our usual station, but Radio Londra, says that the Germans have surrendered at Stalingrad.

"It's a hard winter, and the fishing season won't be starting any time soon," comments the Turk who is listening to the news on the radio with us.

XXV

One morning Mother takes the train with me. She is a sight to see, a real lady, almost like the Lady herself. The caviar Lady I mean. She's put on her shoes with the heels, a really elegant black skirt, silk stockings, and her coat with the angora rabbit collar that she insists on calling "*lapin*", even knowing full well that French is a useless language. We can say the same things in Italian and they even sound better. We are the heirs of the ancient Romans, not descendants of the Gauls. Julius Caesar had no trouble conquering them.

"Yes Nellino, I'm sure you're right," she sighs, clearly bored.

I look at her: she's wearing earrings too, and a string of pearls round her neck. Even a smart hat and a little bag. At home Mother looks very different. Even when she goes into the village I've never seen her dressed up like this.

"Come with me Nellino, be my chaperone."

Actually I would have preferred to talk to Giuseppe who gets the train to school too.

"Where are you going Mother?" I ask.

"Ferrara," she says, coquettishly.

I hate it when she uses that voice. Insufferable woman.

"You're not coming to speak to my teachers, are you?"

"If I have time, maybe I will."

"What do you mean if you have time?"

"Don't you worry about it Nellino, your mother knows what she's doing."

Well, good for her, because I have no idea what my mother is doing on the morning train. She gets back in the evening, much later than me. In good spirits. What the blazes...?

"Why are you singing Mother?"

"I've had a good day."

"What for?"

"Give me a rose to hold on my heart... tie it with your golden hair..."

"Come on Mother, why won't you tell me what you were doing in Ferrara today and why you're so happy?"

"Maybe tomorrow you'll cry... but then will come a smile..."

"Would you just stop it with that singing and tell me!"

"Who is Lilì Marleen?" Mother continues, as if I was invisible.

"Who is Lilì Marleen?" now Uncle's gone and joined in too.

They're making fun of me with all this stupid singing.

"Your Mother is happy," says Uncle, "because she went to talk to Aldo."

"Who?"

"The boy who helps the errand boy."

"Ah yes, the errand boy's assistant. The one with all the freckles. And what's so important about him that Mother's all done up in her Sunday best?"

"He's going to come and work with us," Mother chirps.

"Who's us?"

"Us and our caviar factory."

When she says this, in my mind's eye I get a picture of a hand-painted sign in the centre of the village: Scaramagli Brothers, Prized Po Caviar. I can see the colors too, gold writing on a red background. Or maybe black would be better, black like the sturgeon's eggs, like the Fascist shirt. I like what I see... a delivery truck full of mahogany chests proudly emblazoned with our name, ready to be sent by train to Switzerland, Germany, America, even to the English who are bombing us. Anywhere there are cosmopolitans with money... I'm so lost in this daydream that I don't realise I'm talking out loud.

"What did you say?" Uncle asks curiously.

XXVI

Mother and Uncle are making plans.

I'm still studying and going to school where Cavicchi tells me that I should care less about Aeneid and more about war bulletins. When I ask him why, he answers me quite rudely:

"Can't you see that everyone's screwing us over?"

"There's no need to be so rude! Studying classics is important!"

"You're a real idiot Scaramagli."

Every time I want to ask him why, Boldini, the supply teacher, tells us to be quiet. After school I'm running to catch the train when I hear a voice calling my name:

"Nello! Nellino from the station!"

Who on earth can be calling my name here in Ferrara? I turn round and see a dark-colored car, and for a moment it reminds me of the one they took Salvi away in. Then right away I recognize the Lancia Ardea and see it's the errand boy, smiling and waving at me. Overdoing it a bit, I think. He'll be sweating.

"What a pleasure to see you here."

"What do you mean here? I live in Ferrara."

"Here at school I mean."

“Ah yes, I was just passing and I thought that maybe you would enjoy a ride in the car.”

“Where to?”

“To the station, the village.”

“Is that where you’re headed?”

“Yes, I want to talk to your mother and see if they’ve any intention to start fishing some sturgeon again and make a little money.”

He rubs his thumb and index finger together in the classic gesture.

“The Turk says that this year the season is late starting.”

“The Turk always has something to say for himself, but times have changed, I’ve no use for an old scaremonger like him. You going to get in?”

“If it’s no trouble,” I venture, never having set foot inside a car before.

“Climb aboard then!” and he opens the door of the Ardea.

Now here’s a taste of luxury, I think to myself. I clamber in awkwardly, my books under my arm.

“Get in, get in. I’ll wager you didn’t know this beauty can do 105 kilometres an hour!”

And as he says it he turns the ignition key and puts the car into gear, and we’re off with a roar. He opens the window and says: “Now just listen to that, my boy!”

I’m too busy being cold with the window down, but I don’t say anything. The errand boy extols the virtues of the Ardea.

“In a tick we’ll be in the village, no need to wait for the train. Do you have any idea of the number of cigarettes I’ve smoked on that station platform? I could stop smoking now if I wanted to, once I’ve got my hands on the wheel there’s nothing else I need. Zang tumb tumb! Do you study Marinetti at school?"

"Erm, no. We're still on Petrarch."

"That old stuff! Now's the time for speed, modernity, technology, machines. This is the future, my boy. You do care about the future, don't you?"

"Yes, of course I do."

"But whose?"

"Italy's."

"It's your own you should be worrying about. Just look, round that corner and you're home."

He's right, it's hardly taken any time at all.

"Thank you."

"Would you tell your mother that I'd like a quick word?"

"Of course."

"Call me Girolamo if you like."

"Mother, Mother, you have a visitor!"

"Who is it?"

"Oh, it's you," she says, not exactly happy to see him.

"I've come to talk to you and your brother."

"Come through then, he's in the station, in the office."

Unseen, I slip into the cubbyhole by the freight office, the perfect spot for hearing what's being said in Uncle's office. Too bad I hadn't noticed it when the Lady used to come...

"Well, this is a fine way to repay me," I hear the errand boy saying.

"What do you mean?" asks Uncle.

"Don't play the fool with me, your sister has been trying to hire Aldo, my assistant."

"It's a free market."

"Nonsense! Betraying someone you've known for years! Is that your idea of a free market? I've always been a friend to you, I've always kept quiet about your relationship with the lady, your dealings, your friends and relatives..."

I had no idea what he was talking about.

"We would've told you when the time was right," Mother interjects.

"Sure, once I was ruined. All I need to do is have a quiet word to the Secret Police and remind them who your son's father is... not to mention our other little agreements..."

Not being able to see anything, I can't tell who he's looking at or see their expressions, so it's hard to work out what's going on. I've never heard the errand boy sound so threatening.

"Don't you go raising your voice to me," says Uncle.

"And you stop trying to pull a fast one on me. I have all of your sister's papers."

"Oh no you don't."

"That means you must have them then..."

"That's enough! Would you two please just stop it now?" Mother cuts in.

"I know you're a reasonable boy... I mean man…," she corrects herself, "a reasonable man, I'm sure we can come to an agreement."

"A gentlemen's agreement," says Uncle.

"A gentlemen's agreement?" says the errand boy. "Actually you're right. I'm growing tired of the caviar business anyway."

"What? You mean you want to leave the business?"

"Nothing of the sort Mrs. Scaramagli! I just mean I'm tired of being up to my elbows in fish guts to make an honest living. I could deal with the sales side of the business."

"And who would make the caviar?"

"Your factory."

"Aldo told you about that too?"

"Of course. Aldo knows where his loyalties lie. There's just one small detail we need to discuss."

"What?"

"That it won't be just your factory, but ours. You supply the workers, as you're good at convincing them. I'll send Aldo and give you the benefit of my experience. And if you need capital I know the right people to go to."

"With a war on?"

"More so than ever. Money is worth less and less these days. Either you spend it on the black market to fill your belly..."

I bite my lip so as not to laugh thinking about the tubby errand boy saying these things.

"Or you can invest it where you're sure of a return. And you can't go wrong with caviar. Everyone wants it. From the Caspian Sea after the strategic retreat from Stalingrad."

"You mean the defeat," Uncle puts in.

"Don't tell me you're a defeatist now Mr. Scaramagli? Don't forget I'm a patriot, a good Fascist and a good Italian."

"Forgive me."

"And we all know that the war can't last forever."

"Ah, of course, I was forgetting that the final victory is always near."

"There's no need to be like that. No-one wants the war, I know people are sick and tired of it. There will be an armistice, you'll see an honorable peace. I know important people who are working on it."

"Well that would make things easier," says Uncle.

"No, it would make everything more complicated, because the Russians would start selling caviar again, so ours would have to be the best. Now we're doing well because we're the only ones selling it."

He's got that sweaty head of his screwed on alright, I think, crouching behind the door.

"I'll have the notary draw up the papers to set up the company. What shall we call it?"

"I don't know."

"Well, seeing as I have some knowledge of the business, we'll call it The Italian Caviar Company, Prized Sturgeon Specialities."

"Isn't that a bit long?" Mother attempts to get her oar in.

"No, no, quite the opposite, the longer it is the more important it sounds. Oh, and I was forgetting. Fifty one percent of the company is mine, the rest is yours."

"But there are three of us, it should be split three ways," Uncle says.

"Are you forgetting what we talked about?"

"No, of course not. As you wish."

"And be sure to tell the Turk it's time to start fishing again. Sooner or later we'll have to get round finding a replacement for him though."

"Why so?"

"He's the old guard. We are the future."

"But he's fifty-two, like me."

"It's his ideas that are old fashioned. But don't you worry about it. You are open minded, and from now on you're the boss."

XXVII

The Turk tells the women. And Mother. And Don Antonio. The season is late starting this year, there's no point going out on the water. But everyone else wants to get started. With the same enthusiasm as the year before, but with a few more black headscarves worn as a sign of mourning, because since the retreat from Stalingrad every so often there has been news of someone's son who has died.

Those in Africa or Greece are not faring much better. I mean I know the war is finished in Greece but every so often someone dies nonetheless. No-one knows why.

Getting to school is more difficult now too: there are hardly any trains these days and it's usually mid afternoon before I get home. Giuseppe, the other student who used to take the train, has moved in with some relatives in Ferrara. The only one who is doing well out of all of this is Remo. Of course, it means he never goes anywhere without a gun, even when he's just working on the railway, but even the nobility are going to him to buy flour, eggs, meat, fish, sugar and coffee these days. People say they come by road, to the other side of the signal box, in cars that are even bigger than Dr. Girardi's Isotta Fraschini. Rumor has it that a countess was seen making eyes at Remo, a duke, fallen on hard times, bartered his coat of arms for a string of sausages, and the drivers of some noble families have brought jewels, gold and silverware to exchange for a couple of capons or a salami. I don't know how much of it is true. But as these stories do their rounds the delights that Remo keeps in his signal box multiply, along with our hunger and the desire to sate it. Some of the women on the river bank say that he'll end up selling caviar too. I know that it'll actually be Mother and Uncle selling the caviar, they just haven't told anyone yet.

I'm a bit disappointed that the factory is not going to be called Fratelli Scaramagli. The river beds have been dredged even more thoroughly this year, the boats are ready, all spick and span, the nets are as good as new and though the women are tired after the harsh winter, they're eager to get out on the river. Don Antonio even sings the *Stabat Mater* to winkle out the more religious sturgeons. But it gets to the tenth of March and they've been out fishing every day for a month and caught nothing.

The only person who has no intention of coming home empty handed is the Turk. He and Nicola go hunting or fishing for pike and in the end they always manage to get their hands on something to sell to Remo, for his rich customers. The sturgeon fleet is all in, the houses and families are going to rack and ruin and there doesn't seem to be any way to turn things round. The women go back and forth to the Turk to ask him the reason why, and he just shrugs his shoulders:

"It's cold this year, and anyway you can never tell with fish."

He's not bothered, but all the others are.

XXVIII

At school Cavicchi tells me that he knows for sure that all the workers in Turin have gone on strike and people are sick to the back teeth of Mussolini and the war. I don't really understand it, everything is getting more and more complicated to figure out for someone like me. I'm just a lad from the provinces, a stationmaster's nephew. When I get home I ask Uncle what a strike is. In the village and on the riverside we have other problems, in any case. Okay, the government, the Duce, the homeland, the king, the war, which is now total, the strikes… that's all well and good. But we have no sturgeons and with no sturgeons there can be no caviar factory. And all the women in the village are cross with Mother. Actually some are plain mad with her, saying that she's got ideas above her station, that she wants to boss everyone around. Others blame the Turk, saying that he's stopping the sturgeons from coming, that he's the devil in person. Then there are others who say it's Don Antonio's fault, while he keeps defending both Mother and the Turk and asking everyone to pray.

"Only curses can save us now! You can keep your prayers to yourself!" Mario's father says to him one day. "This river is cursed, and no-one can see it."

"The sturgeons will come, you'll see, just have faith in the Lord," Don Antonio replies.

"The Lord's got nothing to do with it. Some years the fish just don't come up the Po, and it looks like this is one of them," the Turk says.

"Nonsense!"

"*Ave Maria...*"

"It'll take more than a prayer."

"*Gratia plena...*"

"Amen to that Father."

"*Dominus tecum...*"

"What we need isn't a rosary," says Don Antonio all of a sudden. "We need to pray to Saint Joseph! Saint Joseph grant us forgiveness for our sins, protection for our children on the front line and mercy for the sturgeon."

But Saint Joseph can't have got the message and takes mercy on the sturgeons instead, making sure none of them land in a net till April. And this despite the fact that on March 19th 1943 a total of thirty-nine boats, all the boats on the riverside apart from the Turk's, line up to pray for mercy to the statue of Saint Joseph that Don Antonio has hoisted into the biggest boat in place of the harmonium. So, while Italian soldiers are dying in Russia and Africa and workers are striking all over Italy, here, in the middle of the Po we are all praying for a fishing miracle.

"Maybe they should have prayed to Saint Sturgeon," Cavicchi points out mischievously when I tell him about it at school.

He tells me the latest on the strikes: they're everywhere now even if the workers are getting sent to jail in their dozens, in their hundreds... He gets the news from a clandestine newspaper his father receives. In the evening he calls them to the table - Andrea, which is Cavicchi's name, his brother, his mother and the maid, and reads the articles out quietly then folds the sheet in four and hands it back to the maid.

"And what does she do with it?" I ask, amazed.

"She takes it to other comrades, I reckon."

Cavicchi calls himself a comrade, which, like strike, is another word I don't know.

"Those who fought for the freedom of Spain, like your father, were comrades," Uncle explains.

"I thought my father was a traitor?"

"That's something you'll have to decide for yourself, when you're older. He was a man with great ideals, ideals that are different from those around today."

"Anyway, today the errand boy came, Nellino. We won't be starting the factory any more. It's April and there have been no fish. I just wanted to let you know."

XXIX

April has always been the best month for fishing. The month that can sort things out or turn a bad year good. But this April there are hardly any boats left on the river. Almost all of the women are back on the riverside. They go out foraging for salad leaves instead, so at least they have something to put on the table. The Turk and Nicola fish for perch, and they even bring us some one night, a cause for great celebration.

"It's not time for sturgeons yet," the Turk insists.

Meanwhile the huts on the riverside are filling with new inhabitants. Families from the city, where it seems to be more difficult to get by. Here you can only tell that a war's on and that it's not going very well because of the rationing and the black aprons worn by the women in mourning. Otherwise it would just be spring. Cavicchi gives me more calamitous news than Radio Londra about the Italian forces at the front. Apparently we're losing in Africa as well as Russia. Honorably, of course, but losing nonetheless. It's much worse than they say on the radio, which we don't really trust any more anyway.

Halfway through the month Nicola comes to the railway station:

"I've come to send a telegram."

"Who to?" I ask, because like everyone else I don't believe the sturgeons are going to put in an appearance this year.

"To the Lady, I mean the errand boy. Forty-four kilos, female." Nicola looks at me and smiles.

"Good work!" I want to say.

But instead I just return his meaningful look. Nicola has become a man.

"How's life down on the riverside?"

"Fine. Haven't seen you for a while though, not even to read poems to Bechi."

"Give us a hug," I say.

"Ferrara's turned you into a fairy, has it?"

"Ah come on. Even the Roman Centurions hugged their friends."

"Fairies the lot of them."

"Listen to you!"

"Do you know what my father says? He says that if the war doesn't end soon we'll get called up too."

"But I'm only fifteen this year."

"Yeah, next month."

"It was your birthday a few days ago, wasn't it?"

"Yep, you've got a good memory."

"Do you remember that day we caught the eel man's eels?"

"How could I forget it? Anyway my father says that they'll lower the age of conscription if the war goes on and they'll call us up at sixteen."

"Don't talk rubbish! The war's almost over anyway."

"Says who?"

"The errand boy. I listened in one time he was talking about having friends in high places."

"So you're spying on people now?"
"No! It was just that time."
"I'm off home."
"I'll go and send your telegram."

The Turk and the other men who have boats out start catching a few sturgeons, and some of the women whose husbands are at the front get their boats out too. The errand boy doesn't come by in his Lancia Ardea any more, but sends Aldo by train. There are hardly any trains now. And Aldo has time to smoke all the cigarettes he could want waiting for the Littorina or steam train. It looks like the season is going to come good, but one day Maria and her daughter Magda catch something in their net that doesn't struggle like a fish but drags instead.

"The boat is getting dragged out into the middle of the river," Nicola tells me, "and those poor creatures are shouting: 'Turk! Turk! We've got a big fish but it's not tiring and the current's pulling it away.' So we go over to them and my father jumps into their boat. He starts pulling and pulling and you can see that whatever it is is not moving like a fish. And in the end..." Nicola makes the sign of the cross. "It was a dead body that was tangled up in the net. It was all swollen up and just the sight of it made me puke my guts up. I mean I would have puked up if I'd had anything in my stomach, there's hardly anything to eat even in the country now."

"But who was it?"

"Who knows? The Carabinieri came to take him away. They asked us a few questions and then they told us to be more careful, as if we were actually going out looking for dead bodies."

XXX

Looking or not, it is not long before the fourth body shows up, and one even has a good iron anvil tied round its neck. The women begin to say that people are better off staying at home than fishing up dead bodies. Mario's dad is okay till the third one, when he spits on the ground and says that if he'd wanted to be an undertaker he would have gone to work in a graveyard. The fish isn't selling any more. There's no problem with the eggs, and the errand boy is not bothered by the dead bodies: "As long as I'm still alive what should I care?"

"The people round here are saying that the sturgeon have a curse on them, that they'll end up bringing pestilence and disease."

"Let them talk, Pompeo. The people who eat our caviar are hardly going to know that we're fishing dead bodies out of the Po too."

No-one knows where all the corpses are coming from. The Carabinieri take them away and don't even ask any more questions, as if it was normal to be picking up dead bodies like that. Nicola says that if it carries on like this he'll be spending more time in the police station reporting bodies than out on the river. And nobody wants our fish any more. The broker says that the news is doing the rounds. Even Remo, who in the beginning used the dead bodies as an excuse to lower his prices, lays it on the line: "No-one wants fish from the Po any more. People say there's a curse on them. I can't even give it away."

And it's true. The Turk, for the first time since I've known him, takes a sturgeon and roasts it over an open fire. He invites all the inhabitants of the riverside to partake, but half of them don't go, even though they're all famished. That was when he decided that enough was enough: "It's not worth fishing for sturgeon any more. We can eat roach, tench, perch and eel - fish you can catch without pulling up someone with their throat cut."

The errand boy turns up in his Lancia Ardea, parking right at the top of the embankment and almost rolling down to the riverside, shouting:

"Turk, Turk, if you stop fishing you'll bankrupt me!"

"Like you would think twice before ruining me?"

The errand boy is left speechless. Then he recovers: "Name your price."

"Go and ask the others if they want to be corpse fishers in the river. I've had enough of pulling in bodies with their throats cut..."

He's not going to budge and the errand boy gives up without a fight. Partly because everyone knows how stubborn the Turk is. And partly because the season is almost over and most of it has already gone to pot. And partly because he has made arrangements with other fishermen in the Delta, less scrupulous than the Turk, but as the errand boy says, more businesslike. It's Aldo that tells Mother, they've been friends for a while now.

There is no news about the dead bodies. Only Cavicchi at school has some theories, that he gets from the newspaper his family reads at home. Apparently there are political groups that oppose Fascism, Communists or something, who are fighting the government.

"So they're against our soldiers?"

"No, they're against the servants of power."

"Who?"

"One day I'll explain."

The ones ending up in the Po would appear to be the victims of actions against Fascism, against the government and against the war.

"That's why the Carabinieri aren't saying anything," concludes Cavicchi. "They know who the bodies are. It's the rest of us who have to be kept in the dark."

"Cavicchi! Scaramagli! Stop talking or I'll separate you," shrieks Mrs. Boldini.

I don't know how Cavicchi manages to think all these things at once at the age of fifteen, but I think he might be right. Though he does like to lay it on thick with me. By now the sturgeon season is over and fortunately we are well into the school year too.

XXXI

There aren't that many books at home any more. I think Uncle sold a few of his to buy the ones I need for school. None of us has made any money out of the caviar. Nothing more than a few beans to make it easier to scrape by.

"You win some you lose some. It's like gambling in the casino," says the Turk, who takes his boat out of the water in June.

"The water is dirty now too. They're dumping stuff from the factories."

"But there's nothing left in the factories."

"I'm telling you there's muck going into this river. I don't drink the water any more," says Nicola.

I never have, I think. The river is no longer the wonderful place it used to be. There's something going on that we don't understand. It's a bit like what's happening to me – I've got a face full of yellow zits. The worst ones are the neck ones, because I've started shaving and the razor blade often slices the top off them, spraying blood and pus everywhere. It's really gross.

"It's nothing to worry about, it's quite normal at your age," Mother says.

It might well be normal at my age but getting blood on

the mirror is hardly nice. And I'm no great shakes in the mirror stakes either. My hair is getting less blonde and more red. When I say so to Mother she looks at me sternly and says:

"I don't know what you're talking about!"

Just what I see. Under my skin, which is still as white as ever, I can see freckles rising up, not faint ones like Uncle has, but great big dark ones like Aldo's. Cavicchi has taught me how to cup my hand to check if my breath smells. Apparently smelly breath sends the girls running.

"Uncle can I use your Brylcream?" I shout from the bathroom.

"Yes, but don't overdo it, and get a move on! You've been in there for an hour and there are people waiting."

"Thanks Uncle, I'm almost done," I shout back. I rub some Brylcream between my hands, and spread it over my hair to try and flatten it down, but it keeps springing back up again. I slick it back with a fine-toothed comb - Cavicchi told me it's the best way to get a smart side parting. My hair starts sticking up all over the place and I think it's going to take more Brylcream. I hope Uncle isn't going to get mad. Okay, that should do it.

"Nellino can you please come out! I want to go to mass!" Mother raps imperiously on the door, sounding annoyed.

"I'm coming! Just a second!"

"That's what he said to me twenty minutes ago," Uncle remarks.

"Oh well, he's just a boy."

"Just as well! If he was a girl I'd have to wash at the station pump!"

"Oh, don't be sarcastic Pompeo."

"And you stop spoiling him. You don't think he's got a girlfriend, do you?"

"My little Nellino?" Mother bursts out laughing.

I take offence at this and my hair springs up all over again.

At last I'm standing in front of the bookcase with my glasses on and my hair slicked back, in the very latest style. Like a man. Oh fiddlesticks! I hadn't thought about the bike ride, which will no doubt put my hair right back to square one again. How on earth am I ever going to look good?

"What are you looking for Nellino?" Uncle surprises me, lost in thought, standing in front of his books.

"Poems."

"Aha! So you do have a girlfriend!" he chuckles.

"What? Just because I want a poem or two..."

"Poetry is the stuff of young love, you know."

"That's not true! Carducci wrote for the King!" I shoot back, but I can feel myself going red.

"Don't start with all your stories about king and country, the empire, Mussolini and all that jazz. Times have changed."

I would like to say that times have changed for me too, and I know what he means, but I can't work myself up to it. After all I'm still an *Avanguardista* in the Fascist Youth Movement and I try not to miss too many Saturdays. Mr. Masini the physical education teacher told me that for my school career it's important to be seen in the right places.

"Certain absences will be noted," he said, looking me up and down.

The problem is that I can't find the book I'm looking for. But I know it was here. I saw it not that long ago.

"Perhaps I know what you're looking for," says Uncle, with a conspiratorial air. "Come with me."

We go downstairs, into the stationmaster's office. Uncle gets out his big bunch of keys and opens a drawer.

"It's there, John Keats is there..."

"But how did you know this is what I was looking for?"

"Once I tried to win a girl's heart the same way."

"And how did it go?"

"Aha! So there is a girl!"

"No, no, I was just wondering, that's all."

"Fill for me a brimming bowl..." Uncle starts reciting, "And in it let me drown my soul, But put therein some drug, designed... To banish Women from my mind."

"It sounds like it didn't go well."

"No, it didn't."

"But do you know the whole book off by heart?"

"Just a few poems. And how do you know it?"

"Cavicchi told me to read it, actually he recommended it." I bite my tongue to shut myself up.

"So he recommended it to impress a girl," Uncle concludes, teasing me. "Do I know her?"

"I've got to go."

"Off you go then."

"Just one thing Uncle..."

"What?"

"Why do you keep the book hidden like that?"

"I don't really know. I just think that these days it's better not to have an English poet in your bookcase."

Or carry one with you, I think, covering up the book in a page of *Il Corriere della Sera*. It'll protect it too. When I get to the riverside, my hair is still almost presentable. In front of the Turk's house I put my glasses on, clear my throat loudly and knock on the door...

"Come in!"

"But you don't even know who it is!"

"It's you Nellino, I saw you on your bicycle up on the embankment."

"Are Nicola and his father not in?"

"No, they're out fishing for frogs."

I know this, and it's why I've come now. I don't tell Bechi that but she might have worked it out for herself. I stop in the middle of the dirt floor room which functions as hallway, kitchen, workshop and storeroom, basically the daytime part of the house, where a girl like Bechi can go so far as to invite in an old family friend. I can feel the blood rushing to my temples. I don't say anything. I open the book at the page Cavicchi told me and start reading. He told me to pluck up the courage so I do:

"You say you love; but with a voice..."

My voice cracks a little at this, but I take a deep breath, look up from the page and hear the words echoing:

"Chaster than a nun's, who singeth
the soft Vespers to herself
While the chime-bell ringeth
O love me truly!"

When I get to the bit that says "love me" I think I'm going to faint, but at least I've plucked up my courage. I feel brave but I'm sweating. Worse than the errand boy. Now I'm afraid Bechi is going to burst out laughing, but what I really hope is that she sheds a tear or two, and says "My hero, I…"

Or at least does something.

But I look at her and she's smiling, happy, like a little girl.

I'm about to tell her that the poet is called Keats, John Keats, when she opens her mouth and I hear a sound that arranges itself into the words:

"How fever'd is the man! Who cannot look…" she takes a breath and looks at me:

"Upon his mortal days with temperate blood,
Who vexes all the leaves of his life's book,
And robs his fair name of its maidenhood."

No way! This is just not fair! How is it that everyone here knows Keats off by heart as if it was boring old Arnaldo Fusinato with disease raging and no bread left.

So much for Cavicchi. He told me she would fall at my feet! That my culture and my glasses and John Keats would win her over in a flash. What a buffoon, I think. I'm the only one round here who has to read Keats from the book, everyone else has it at their fingertips.

"Oh Nellino," says Bechi, who can see that I am a bit downhearted, to say the least. "What a lovely surprise! John Keats is one of my favorite poets."

"But... but... How do you know him? I mean you're always here, on the riverside."

"I've got a book of his, my Aunt left it to me."

"The Turk has a sister?"

"No, I mean yes, another aunt..."

Now I've embarrassed her.

"Sorry."

"No, I'm sorry. But do you think this is the kind of poem you should be reading to an unchaperoned girl?"

It's because you're unchaperoned that I read it, I should have answered. Instead I say that I was foolish.

"You're still a child, Nellino, what are you doing thinking about love?" Bechi murmurs, ruffling my hair.

"Oh my goodness! What have you put on your hair?" she asks, sniffing her fingers.

"Brylcream."

Bechi bursts out laughing: "What? Like the mayor, the chemist and all those gentlemen who give themselves airs round here?"

"No! It's not like that. It's really fashionable you know. And it's not mine, it's Uncle's."

"See what I mean, it's what old men use."

"You look really nice with your hair like that," I say, looking at my shoes.

"Thank you, but please no more compliments, or I'll have to ask you to leave."

"Do you mind if I read you another poem?"

"No, not at all, that would be lovely. I don't know the whole book off by heart you know."

"You know, this year we're working hard at school, especially with Greek and Latin, but I'm really glad of it. It's a real shame you and Nicola can't go to school."

"Well, we do what we can. But let's not talk about sad things, life is hard enough already. Read to me Nellino, read me something nice."

I look at her, in clogs with no stockings, and a dress that looks like a work smock with the cuffs that droop down over her hands. Her hands are beautiful, with long, tapering fingers. They might be rough because of doing all the housework, but they still look like the hands of a pianist. Under the dress is her chest, and I can almost make out the shape of it, but her dress is so loose it keeps temptation at bay.

But my gosh I feel tempted all the same, when I look at her slender neck, her soft ears, her dark hair, her dark, sparkling eyes, her mouth...

"Are you going to start reading or are you just going to stand there staring at me all day?"

That's my Bechi, the feisty Bechi who's at home on the riverside - part young lady, part fishing companion. What I really want to ask her is whether it's true she kissed Nicola. But instead I read. She sits and listens for a bit, then she stands up and says:

"That's enough for now, I have to make lunch."

"I'll help you if you want."

"You already did that once and remember how it turned out."

She's talking about the time I tried to help her clean the floor.

"I slipped..."

"It doesn't matter, it was nice of you to try, but now you should go."

"You're sure I can't help you?"

"No. It's really not suitable for a boy and a girl to spend such a long time in the house together, unchaperoned. It's only because we're in a war that these kinds of things can happen. Give my regards to your family, Nellino."

"And you give mine to the Turk and Nicola."

"You don't go fishing or hunting or anything with him any more. He misses you, you know."

"Says who?"

"He does."

"Really?"

"Really."

"Then tell him that this afternoon, if he wants a bike race, I'll come by: we can go to a creek on the other side of the Po that's full of catfish."

"They catch catfish here too you know."

"Yeah, well, tell him I'll come, on my bike."

"Thank you, Nellino."

"Thank *you*, doll," I wish I'd replied, before putting my arm round her waist and kissing her passionately.

"You're welcome," I say, instead. And I leave.

XXXII

There's a military train on the way. It's a troop train going to Lombardy, Uncle tells me, but it's a secret. It's strange, I think, because the Americans and the British are in Sicily, we should be going South to fight.

"It'll be a convoy of troops coming home from the Russian front," Uncle murmurs.

"Not from Africa?"

"It doesn't look like anyone's coming back from Africa."

"What do you mean Uncle?"

"They're all prisoners. If they're not dead."

Well, I'd like to talk to the soldiers on the train, embrace them, shout Long Live Italy and raise the flag. To let them know that we're with them and that sometimes wars can be lost too. Because all wars are wrong. That's what my father used to say, Mother tells me when I ask her why we are losing the war when we're in the right.

"Nobody is in the right during a war because all wars are wrong."

"What are you talking about Mother? What about the wars of independence that united Italy?"

"I don't know Nellino, maybe those had to be done, but I'm

not the only one who thinks these things, it's what your father thought, he often said it."

"But I thought he died in a war?"

"Well, maybe he thought his war was a just one, just like you think the wars of independence are."

"This war is right too, Mother, and it will make Italy great."

"No, Nellino, this is not a just war, because all it's doing is making us poorer. And killing people's sons far from home."

Mother's wrong. Well, she's right about us having to tighten our belts, but our men in Russia and Africa fought valiantly. They still deserve a hero's welcome. Unfortunately they're making them travel at night, when it's dark. And they have orders not to stop in any stations. Uncle got a telegram saying the transit of the military train is confidential. But he tells me about it nonetheless. And I go out onto platform 1 at 2.35 in the morning when the troop train is going to be passing through. At first I think I'll wave at them through the windows, then I think that this calls for more than just a handkerchief. A flag is what's needed. There's one in the office, so I go to get it. Uncle is already on the platform with his light to give them the signal to pass through. I think he's excited too because we hardly ever get long trains coming through our station. But now for some unknown reason they are sending lots of convoys on our line, almost always freight, by which I mean military freight. But this is the first troop train. It puffs in, not going that fast, but doesn't slow down. Uncle raises his arm. I see the wagons rolling past me and I'm about to raise the flag...

"But it's a German train..."

"Yes, they're our allies Nellino."

Suddenly I don't feel like hoisting the flag or even waving it any more. The train does not displace enough air to make the flag flutter, and it hangs limply on its pole.

"Those bloody bastards!" I hear Uncle cursing under his breath.

"What happened?"

"They nearly took my arm off! If I hadn't given them the signal it would have been all the same to them. Acting like they own it all. Allies my foot!"

And whose allies are they anyway? The next day I find out that we don't even have a government any more. Well, I mean we do, but it's complicated. In the morning I take the train to Ferrara: this year in July the teachers are giving extra lessons for free to bring us up to speed for fifth year. It's Mrs. Boldini's idea. She hasn't got a husband so it's not like she's going to take a holiday. The headmaster was over the moon. Basically school is going to go on for another month. I don't really need extra lessons, but from the sounds of things those who don't take them will have a hard time of it next year. As it's shorter hours, Cavicchi comes to the station to get me and we walk to school together. Today, however he is all worked up about something, and comes rushing over to me:

"Have you heard the news? Mussolini has been arrested! That'll put an end to this sham. Let Hitler have a total war if that's what he wants."

"Andrea! What are you talking about?"

"It happened yesterday. I heard it on the radio."

"But I was up in the night and I never heard anything."

"Being up isn't enough, you actually have to turn on the radio, genius. It was on the news at a quarter to eleven."

"No-one on the train said anything about it."

"Take a look here," he says, showing me the newspaper.

"Hells bells! The King's in charge of the army?"

"Yes! And Badoglio is in charge of the government. No school for us today, my friend. You can come to my house."

"To your house?"

"Yeah, go on. Not even Boldini will be in school today. And I want you to meet my parents. I've already told them you'll come. It's summer after all - we should be on holiday anyway."

"No, I don't want to be any trouble. Really."

"Of course you won't be."

"Well, I don't want to."

"What? Don't you like the idea?"

"Yes, a bit, but..."

I'm not sure how things are going to develop and I think I'd better go home, but the first train isn't till the afternoon.

"Alright then, I'll come."

XXXIII

"So you're Menandro Costa's son? I have to say there is a certain resemblance... When Andrea told me I couldn't believe it. A young Costa! Let me see you. Oh, and do come in, pleased to meet you, Lorenzo Cavicchi."

"My pleasure, Nello Scaramagli. Scaramagli, not Costa."

"Of course, sorry, Andrea told me your father didn't give you his name."

"No, he wasn't around long enough."

"Ah yes! Travelling the world for his ideals, eh? Well, it was high time Italy put an end to this regrettable interlude and the king took the country under control again. The country's on its knees and we're overrun with oafish Germans. Just think that the other day I was talking to an SS officer who didn't even know who Weill was! 'What?' I said to him: 'One of the greatest living German composers!' 'I have never heard of him. He cannot be German.' That's what he said."

"Actually I've never heard of him either."

"Andrea, what are you teaching our young guest?"

"It's not like me and Nello talk about absolutely everything, Father. And Kurt Weill is Jewish after all - it doesn't seem like the best time to be waving it in the face of a German soldier."

"They'll all have to go back home now anyway."

"Actually last night it looked like they were going in the opposite direction."

Before I could help myself I'd blurted it out. If only I knew when to keep my mouth shut.

"What are you talking about Nello?"

"No, it was nothing."

"Go on, you can trust us."

Well, who cares now anyway? It's all over and knowing something important makes me feel important in this house that is so big that if I leave the lounge I'll get lost.

I don't tell them about the flag, but about the German train.

"You must have got mixed up," says Cavicchi senior.

"Actually no."

"But that's impossible, a train full of Germans, in Italy, going towards Lombardy, when they have all those other fronts to be sending soldiers to."

"Did you really know my father?"

"Of course, we were together in Spain. Sugar in your coffee?"

But how can it be? In front of me is a renegade, a traitor, like my father, and he's friendly, smiling, jovial, comfortably sitting in an armchair. Or rather sunk into it. I've spent my life being called the son of a traitor. While Andrea Cavicchi, that scoundrel... I've confided in him and he not only goes and tells his father everything, but knows things about me and doesn't even tell me. There's too much going on right now and I don't understand at least half of it.

"But my father was a subversive, a traitor, a renegade..."

It comes out in a childish tone of voice, and I feel like I'm going to cry, but I don't want to.

Mr. Cavicchi looks at me in amazement.

Andrea intervenes: "I told you, Father. They've brainwashed him."

"I didn't think it was to this extent. I'm afraid you've been given the wrong idea about your father," Mr. Cavicchi says, very gently, in a steady, calm voice. The voice of a proper father, I think. I start crying and he gathers me into an embrace. I hear him muttering...

"Your father was a great man... A man who fought for freedom, equality, justice... An anarchist, a cosmopolitan..."

"Like the people who buy the caviar?" I ask.

It's like floodgates have opened in my brain.

"What?"

I can see he hasn't understood. Either that or I haven't.

"No, no, it's nothing."

I stop there.

We spend the morning talking about my father. Then Cavicchi's mother, Maria Luisa, arrives. The maid tells me she's a countess but doesn't use the title, having a Communist for a husband and all. So there it is: this big house in the city centre is the only place in the world where I've heard people talk about Communists, anarchists, freedom, equality and goodness knows what, as if it was the price of milk. That's another thing that doesn't seem to be an issue here, as far as I can see. To be honest, I don't think anything is in short supply in this house.

"Will you be partaking of our humble repast?" Cavicchi's mother drawls.

"Erm..." I gawp at her.

"She means lunch," Andrea comes to my aid.

"Oh, right. Actually no, I can't, I'm sorry, I have to get my train."

"You'll have missed it by now," Andrea shoots back, triumphantly.

I look at the time on the big grandfather clock. It's true. Forget school, the morning here has flown.

"I'll get my brother to take you home on his motorcycle," Andrea adds. "Go on, stay for lunch."

So I do. Judging from the house I imagined lunch would be a more lavish affair, but Mr. Cavicchi says it is important to dominate the appetite, *mens sana in corpore sano* and all that. Which translates into a measly vegetable broth grandly called consommé, and hot to boot, even though it's summer, with no bread, and some boiled potatoes. Just like at home, in other words, or worse. Except at home there are no paintings, portraits of ancestors, tapestries, stuffed deer, armchairs, pianos and maids.

"You know," says Mr. Cavicchi to his wife, "Menandro was so faithful to the ideal that he didn't even give Nello his surname..."

"Oh you poor boy! How on earth do you get by without a surname?" murmurs the decountessed countess.

"Of course he has a surname, dearest scatterbrain. It's just that it's his uncle's, his mother's brother."

"So what's this ideal about then?" I ask tentatively.

"No gods, no masters, my boy."

What that's got to do with surnames I'd like to know, but don't ask. Enrico comes in, Andrea's big brother who is studying engineering in Milan and who this morning decided not to take the train to go on holiday in the mountains, so he could see how things would unfold, Mr. Cavicchi explains.

"Have you ever ridden on a motorcycle?"

"No, I don't think so."

"Okay, well get in the sidecar then, it's safer. And put these on."

He hands me a leather helmet and a pair of goggles. They're enormous.

"Cover your mouth to keep out the dust."

He doesn't give me any advice on how to keep my repast down, and the only reason I don't spew up round every bend is that the consommé and potatoes are long gone.

"Let's give this chap a run for his money!" Enrico bellows every time we overtake someone.

He toots a kind of horn and revs the engine that makes a sound like a tank. At least, I've never heard a tank, but I imagine that's what one would sound like. We have to shout to make ourselves heard.

"My old man'll end up in jail sooner or later," Enrico hollers.

"Why?"

"All that talk about Communism, worse than the bloody Russians!"

Uncle is hardly ever on the street side of the station. He's on the other side, where the tracks are, but in the time it takes for Enrico to park and say goodbye to me, engine running all the while, I see him rushing through, dressed in his stationmaster's uniform.

"We thought something had happened to you."

"I missed the train."

"These days they are few and far between."

"And who was that on the motorcycle?"

"Enrico Cavicchi."

"Your classmate? He's old enough to have a motorcycle?"

"No, no, it's his big brother."

"Ah, the engineer..."

"How do you know?"

"Well, the Cavicchis are a big name in Ferrara."

That may be, but it feels like everyone else knows more than I do here.

"Hi Mother."

"Nellino!"

I'm barely inside the door and she's hugging me, laughing, crying.

"I've been so worried," she whispers.

"What about?"

"That something had happened to you. It's been a strange kind of day."

"What happened?"

"Look over there."

On the other side of the tracks there's smoke rising from the signal box.

"People came looking for Remo, from the fields, or the riverside. 'See what's happened to that Mussolini of yours?' they said. Then they were all kicking and spitting."

"What did Uncle do?"

"Nothing."

"And the railway Militia?"

"Nothing."

"The Militia is part of the army, as of today."

"They only went to send them away when they saw that the

shed behind Remo's house was on fire. The Carabinieri are there now. You go and have a wash now, you look like you've been in the Siege of Jarabub with all that dust..."

"No gods, no masters..."

"What did you say?"

"Nothing, just something I heard."

"What thing?"

"No gods, no masters..."

"You too? Isn't one in the family enough?"

"So it's true then."

"What's true?"

"That this is what my father believed in."

"Yes, that and other things too," Mother says gently.

"How come you never told me?"

"You're the one who never wanted to talk about it. Now run along and get washed. And stop worrying yourself with these things."

"No gods, no masters..."

"Stop it now, silly!"

XXXIV

I thought I'd seen it all, more was yet to come. On September 8th Italy signed the armistice and since then it's felt like the world and his wife are passing through here. Down on the riverside and here in the station. School hasn't started yet, but the war has finished, or at least that's what they're saying on the radio. Cavicchi would know the score, but I haven't seen him since the extra lessons ended.

Since then it's been summer here: the usual mosquitoes, a gnawing feeling of hunger in my stomach, that feels emptier and emptier, a great deal of hustle and bustle in the station, some railwaymen thinking about going on strike and all the villagers conveniently forgetting they used to be Fascists. Comrade Baffoni, first and foremost, who has even reverted to the "lei" form of address with Uncle now when we go to get our hair cut. In the space of a month everything is different. The only person who doesn't seem to have changed his tune is Remo, who still manages to get hold of all the best food.

"You can get anything if you've got the money," Mother comments, with a hint of bitterness.

I reckon she had really been counting on the sturgeon season and the factory because since that went wrong she hasn't smiled a lot. And she never sings. Me and Nicola are friends again, at least for the fishing. The Turk always manages to wangle it so that I am never alone with Bechi, and when I turn up at their place he always gives me some job to do.

We manage to survive the mosquitoes and every so often I bring Mother home a carp to roast, or a barbel, or a porcupine, which isn't a fish but we come across them now and then and Uncle loves the meat. Mother is never overjoyed, because it's a lot of work: you have to pull out all the quills that always prick your hands, then get rid of the skin, and the blood, then it needs to be hung, then...

"I know, I know, Mother. I won't bring them any more."

"That's not what I said. Uncle loves them."

It's a habit of hers, this business of saying something and then pretending she didn't mean it. The solution, when I'm lucky enough to catch more than one, is to take the porcupines to Remo's wife. If I give one to her in exchange she prepares the others. One afternoon by the river while Nicola is working on the boat, which is grounded, and I am telling him about the ancient Egyptians, a real passion of his, a group of Italian soldiers comes along. They don't have weapons, but are in uniform, or what's left of it - rags, more like. Unshaven, with accents from the other side of the Po. When the Turk goes out to greet them they tell him that they've come from the pontoon bridge.

"Can you take us across the river in your boat?"

"No, you can see for yourself that it's grounded."

"We're willing to use force," says one of them, who might be a corporal, and is the leader of the group.

"That boat is staying right where it is," growls the Turk.

Tough man talk. He even looks bigger, and you can tell he has a strength that is unthinkable for a man of his age, which is fifty-two. That's what Uncle says, talking about their generation.

"Why don't you go over the bridge? If it's the toll that's the problem we can give you a hand. I'll get someone to take you, we know the keeper well. For soldiers I'm sure he'd turn a blind eye."

"The problem is not the toll-keeper. It's the Germans."

"The Germans?"

"The bridge is guarded by German soldiers and we don't know if we're still allies..."

"To be honest," another soldier adds, "we don't even want to be soldiers any more. The war's over and we just want to go home."

The Turk is perplexed and offers them a glass of wine.

"Take a seat, let's have a look."

He gives me and Nicola a quick glance that means we've to go and do a recce. We get to the embankment above the bridge. We don't even need to go down, because at the start of the bridge we can see a real-life checkpoint with Germans guarding it. Nicola runs to tell his father, and I go to warn Uncle. But Uncle is all too aware of the situation already: there are Germans in the station too. They have taken over the freight office and have told Uncle he is to collaborate to keep the railway running in good order. I cycle up as fast as I can, but I can see for myself right away, when I see military vehicles parked in front of the station. But I can't work out why. If the war is over, if we've signed the armistice, what do the Germans want with us? Today, as I find out later, they are freeing Mussolini at Gran Sasso. The station is no longer ours either.

I need to speak to Cavicchi about this. So I tell Uncle that I want to go to Ferrara to look for Andrea. He shakes his head:

"You're staying right here."

Then he looks me straight in the eye: "That name, Cavicchi, don't say it here any more, and don't say it in the station again."

I'm not sure I understand why, but I know that I'm scared now.

XXXV

It's very hard to speak to the Germans, but Uncle has a go. He also tries in English, because he reckons he's good at it, but it has a disastrous effect, and almost gets him arrested. In the end they speak to him in Italian. Actually there's only one that speaks to him, an NCO of some kind, maybe a corporal, who says his name is Kraus or something like that:

"Stationmaster! Today two trainz must arrife and vee must check zee passenchers of zee civil convoy."

But if Kraus isn't there guarding the station, to us it's just guttural sounds barking orders.

Luckily they are polite to Mother. Uncle looks at me, dejected.

"Forget Latin and Greek, you should be studying German at school."

"Don't you worry Pompeo, from now on I'll be here to talk to the Germans and everything will be easier."

The voice comes through the glass door of the office which is always open as autumn is late in coming this year. The voice is Remo's, but it's not the usual Remo. He's standing there, all puffed up, hands on his sides, legs slightly apart, smiling with all thirty-two teeth. If he had that many, obviously. Twenty-five would be closer to the mark.

"Afternoon Remo," Uncle says.

He's wearing a uniform that looks new, but against the light it's hard to see. Remo Sacchini, we learn that day, has been transferred from the railway to the Militia, or rather what is shortly to be known as the National Republican Guard. The Republic is that of Salò. I don't even know where it is.

"School should be starting as usual soon," he says, to reassure me. "I'll look after the Germans, I mean our German allies. And you keep the trains running."

"Passenger or military?" asks Uncle with a sarcastic tone he doesn't manage to hide.

"Both," answers Remo, lighting up a cigarette.

"At headquarters," he adds casually, "they told me that I stand a good chance of getting the flat above the station. Of course, I said to myself, it would be good accommodation, but Comrade Scaramagli lives there. So you can see we have all the more reason to cooperate amicably. As a token of my good will I have taken the liberty of bringing you some sugar."

And to Uncle he hands not a twist, but a whole, one-kilo pack of sugar from the sugar plant. Uncle gapes. I think that he's going to insult Remo, kill him, spit in his eye for talking like that. But all he says is: "Thank you Remo, you shouldn't have taken the trouble."

"It's no trouble at all, I assure you."

Remo raises his arms and clicks his heels. Uncle raises his arm too. So basically nothing has changed. He's gone back to using "voi" after a couple of months of "lei". From that day we become a military station, with Germans and Republican soldiers guarding the rail infrastructure, as Remo has taken to calling it.

XXXVI

School did not start as usual, as Remo had promised, but on November 8th, more than a month late. And before that Uncle wouldn't let me go to Ferrara. I've had no news of Cavicchi, so it's a relief to see him in class as usual.

"Hey Scaramagli," he says.

I hug him. "Hi Andrea."

Mrs. Boldini coughs to express her disapproval, but says nothing. Anyway the only thing worth saying, or announcing, is that we are going to be spending another school year with no heating.

During lesson time we have to do air raid drill more and more often: we all have to run to the basement, where they have even set up a small chapel for prayers.

And then there are the Jews. Unfortunately the headmaster was being over-optimistic when he said that our classmate Salvi, alias Rimini, was the only Jewish infiltrator in our school. In the fall of '43 they seem to be coming out of the woodwork in the middle school and even in the high school. All these Jews, who in one way or another have managed to make a mockery of the law.

I myself continue to be Aryan, strawberry blonde with blue

eyes. The way I am, it's impossible for me not to be taken as an example. Because not only do the Jews have their own laws to prevent them from mixing with us, but Mussolini, yes the Duce in person, who was arrested but is now in charge again, is saying that they are enemies and foreigners. In our class Rovighi and Ismani get sent away.

"False surnames," says the headmaster curtly.

Not only are they kicked out of school, they are going to be taken somewhere, to some kind of camp, and from there to Germany. Apparently that's where they have the solution for Jews.

But life here is hard enough, and I don't want to think about it.

"We have to get to the bottom of the racial question," says Cavicchi, who is just not interested in talking about Jews.

The murder of the Fascist Federal Secretary just after school started has got us trying to figure out too many things that are pretty hard to understand, as always. The planes that we hear overhead are often enemy ones, but the newspapers and radio say that other cities are being bombed. So when Ferrara gets bombed during the Christmas holidays, all Mother says is that I'm lucky school is shut. Lucky my foot!

The first time I see enemy planes over the Po I am down on the riverside with Nicola. It is an unforgettable sight, planes that people say are American, flying over the river, at the end of the year. They are noisy, solid-looking and enormous. Yet there is one sound missing from all that noise because what Nicola and I are waiting for, squinting up into the sky, is for the Italian fighter planes to show up. Or the German ones. Or the Anti-Aircraft Brigade. But there's nothing. And on the riverside there are no warning sirens. So if a bridge gets bombed you only know about it if you're on it at the time. Seeing them is scary, but also shocking: these enemy planes are so massive and what's more they seem to have complete freedom of the skies. I never thought that they could actually attack us, attack our things, the station and the railway.

But one day we see a formation of smaller aircraft, two or three of which break away and head straight for us. I can see that they're American, bombers I think, and they're coming to bomb our railway! In the station the siren sounds for real. For the very first time it's not just a drill. We rush down to the basement, which up to now was where we kept the Lambrusco. Now it's our salvation. I don't understand how it can be happening. Remo manages to be allocated a Republican machine gun, as he calls it. He has it installed on our kitchen balcony, which is a bit like inviting the enemy to bomb the station.

What's more, Mother has to make coffee for the gunners, and coffee is like hen's teeth these days. And it's not like the gunners manage to hit any enemy planes in any case. There are bombs raining down, and Mother is busy making coffee. Uncle says that the trains should probably not even be running. But they keep going: there are still three trains a day to Ferrara, including the one I take to school.

One day the planes, which are getting lower and lower over the bridges, hit some of the houses on the riverside.

"This war will be the end of us down here on the riverside," says Nicola.

But when the planes start firing at the train with their guns, and we have to stop because there are bombs landing on the line, Nicola admits that it's tough for everyone. Mother would prefer me not to go to school, because the train is a target. But the station is too. So she is resigned to the fact that I keep going.

That year is a horrendous school year. Not to mention the fishing season. There are Germans down on the riverside. They search the huts and question the fishermen. But it's not just Germans. Remo and his lot give them a hand too. They seize all the boats and take them to the pontoon bridge. To make them available. For who, we don't know. They're left there, piled up round a makeshift mooring, where the current often makes them bang together. They really need a longer pontoon. Or fewer boats. Or just to be a bit more careful with other people's things.

"They didn't take ours," Nicola tells me.

"Why not?"

"Because we didn't have it," interjects the Turk, who has heard us. "The Italian soldiers took it, the deserters who came in September."

Oh them, I'd forgotten all about them. Life is going too fast round here, and I've got to study.

XXXVII

"People say there are groups of partisans in your neck of the woods," Cavicchi says one day.

"Groups of what?"

"Anti-fascists."

"Who?"

"Rebels."

"Oh yes, the fugitives. There are posters up in the village asking them to surrender."

"Ah, Nello, sometimes you're such a blockhead."

"What do you mean?"

"Can't you see it's time we got rid of the Fascists and Germans?"

"The way I see it, the English and Americans are trying to get rid of us, bombing us most days like this."

"My father says that if it goes on like this, middle school and high school pupils will get called up too."

"Are you kidding?"

"No, not at all. There are boys getting called up now too. My brother at university got his card in the post."

"What did he do?"

"He ran away."

"He ran away?"

"Yeah, he joined the partisans."

"But how do you know?"

"I just do."

"Scaramagli! Cavicchi!"

Boldini's screech is drowned out by the sound of the siren.

"I'll see about you two later," she says as we all hurry out of the classroom.

The good thing about being in the shelter is that there are girls in there too, and the scaredy cat teachers huddle into the back of the shelter where it's supposed to be safest. So we can basically do what we like. I read. I've decided that reading is my true passion. Girls are too difficult. You have to spend all this time chatting to them and giving them sweet talk, and making them think you're some kind of big shot, then when it's time to make out they say you're too young, or start laughing at you. The ugly ones are the only ones who'll kiss you. It's better down on the riverside where at least they'll show us their knickers.

"They're not all like that," says Cavicchi. "There's one in fourth grade that if you get her in a corner she'll let you get a good feel, and even though she's short she has great knockers."

And he mimes two great balloons on his chest to make his point.

"I don't believe you."

"You can have a go too."

Needless to say, that day never comes.

XXXVIII

Every time I come home from school I look up to see if there are any planes. To be honest I really like seeing them. Much more than the machine gun on the roof. The only time we really get a proper look at them is when we're on the train and they're bombing the line or flying over to Ferrara or the Po. Then you get to see them. On the train there's no siren and no shelter to go to. All you can do is sit there and look up. Or you can try and hide under the wooden benches like some of the women do, as if that's going to save you from a bomb.

We've seen what they did to the pontoon bridge over the Po: it took the Germans a whole week to get the boats sorted again, and there are still bits and pieces of the old pontoon bobbing about in the water. When the Turk looks at the river he says the sturgeons will be gone for good.

"Even if the war ends it'll take two lifetimes to dredge the riverbed. What with the dead bodies and the scrap metal, the fish won't spawn here again. That's the end of that."

He sighs heavily and pulls on his cigarette. He smokes whatever he can find, straw, butts, dried corn husks, or with any luck, a German cigarette or two. Those get shared by four or five people. Having a whole one to yourself is something people dream about.

Like in the station, Remo has had two small machine guns installed on the train. He has been promoted to second lieutenant and is in command of the Railway Guards of the Republic, at least on our line. Those in the know say that Remo bought his rank with bags of sugar and coffee. The machine guns are mounted one up by the driver, the other at the end of the train. So now in addition to the drivers and the controller there are four soldiers on board too. They have helmets. We don't even have those.

XXIX

At home I ask Uncle what he knows about the rebels who, according to Cavicchi, are on our side. "Nothing" he replies curtly. "It's nothing to do with us. Especially not with the army on the balcony and the Germans in the office."

This time I understand, I have been careless with my words. At home, actually, it is no fun these days. It's like being in prison. Mother says so too, but Uncle pretends not to hear. Until the day a plane crashes by the station yard. It's not a bomber, but an Italian fighter that has been shot down. I rarely see Italian and German fighters attacking American and British planes, which are an increasingly common sight these days. When it happened I was at school. I was on the train home but it was ordered to stop half a mile out of the station, so I stomp home in a temper, and then I see the firemen and the flames, real flames, much higher than when they tried to burn Remo's house down. The station is all hustle and bustle, there are even military ambulances with the red cross on the side. Two railway workers and a republican soldier were killed.

Uncle is going mad trying to get Mother to calm down. She's crying and hollering:

"That's it! We're leaving! Do you hear me? I've had enough!"

And leave we do, all of us. We go down to the riverside, to the Turk's. Uncle takes my bike to go to work in the station, so Nicola lends me his rickety old one to get the train to Ferrara. Who could have imagined us ending up like this: the three of us all sleeping together on a straw pallet on the beaten earth floor?

"It's all I have to offer," says the Turk.

And we take it. Here at least the straw is clean, I've heard there are fleas in the other huts on the riverside. At night I can hear Bechi breathing. She sleeps in the same room, but she's the only one with a bed all to herself. Or rather she used to be, because after three nights she offers to share it with Mother. So there are three straw pallets - one for me and Uncle, one for the Turk and Nicola and one for Mother and Bechi. Talk about going up in the world.

But life in this humble shack has a different atmosphere, that I like. First of all, we don't have to put up with Remo, his wife Pasquina and the insufferable twins Benito and Littorio. The village gossips say that the twins are not Remo's, the usual nobody's children. I think that even if they might not be sure he's their father, at least they've got his surname. And there are no Germans here, and no machine gun on the terrace. That's enough to make it nicer.

The real problem, to be honest, is the night-time. It's too quiet and the silence is too loud. Not that it's noisy in the station, but the trains come through and while other people might think they make a racket, it's music to a railwayman's ears. There are no trains down on the riverside. Down here it's all leaves rustling, nocturnal birds, mosquitoes, things jumping, buzzing, crawling, splashing in the river... The silence we have in the station is something they couldn't even imagine.

And then there are the smells. For us, used to coal and burnt fuel oil, it's like another world. When I used to come here to fish, or to visit Bechi and Nicola, I'd never noticed it. Everything smells of something, and the herbs have a whole spectrum of smells of their own: some tangy and pungent, some sweet, others enveloping.

Mother wears a smock all the time. The same kind of smock that Bechi wears. She ties her hair back every day and has the hangdog look of someone who can't take much more. Uncle has brought all his books to the riverside and when his shifts allow he reads, but not in the evening because here, unlike the station, there is no electric light. There's the odd candle, carefully kept and sparingly used. And oil lamps that are empty because there's no oil. Actually, you can get it from Remo but it costs more than cigarettes. In any case it's not Remo doing the black market any more. It's his wife, Pasquina. Now Remo is in charge of the soldiers who are doing the work of the Railway Militia Corps. He has a uniform of good cloth and boots that don't look like they're made out of cardboard, like those the others wear. Or wood, like the clogs we wear on the riverside.

The only time we wear our shoes is when I go to Ferrara and Uncle goes to the station. At school we hear bombs going off every day and even if the planes don't come the sirens sound anyway. There are massive air raids, with lots of planes. They mostly happen at night and in the morning there's new rubble. But formations fly over during the day too. There are hardly any fighter planes left to protect the city and in any case the machine gun bullets can't reach all the huge British and American planes that fly high overhead and drop their bombs. We hear the explosions. And the sound of houses falling down. With all this going on school finishes earlier and by the end of May we are all at home. The fifth grade exams were a piece of cake. We all get into high school no problem. Me and Andrea say our goodbyes. He tells me that they might be leaving Ferrara that summer too, as it's not safe any more.

XL

June 27th. I remember the date. Because we see bombers coming up the Po and think they're going to attack the bridges. But instead they head for the station and bomb the railway. Not like before, when one or two fighters would break away from the main formation and try to hit the line. No, this is a proper attack. Now there are planes coming almost every day and the railway and the station get hit at least once a week. The only person who still has to go to the station is Uncle, who keeps the trains running with a helmet on his head and reports every night that there's less left standing of our home. Not to mention the railway line. One day he tells me that there are no more trains to Ferrara. We don't even know if they'll be back on after the summer. The only people travelling now are Fascists and Germans.

"There are wagons with anti-aircraft machine guns, but we're not taking people any more," he says gloomily.

"It's not your fault," I say.

He is distraught about the railway going to pieces, his railway.

"You know in a way it's partly my fault too," he says. "We should have caught on sooner."

"Caught on to what?"

"Who Mussolini was and where he would lead us. Who certain people were. Last week Remo arrested some boys who were dodging the draft. They hung them in the station after a summary trial. It was Remo and that German corporal who speaks Italian, Kraus, who passed sentence. They were in front of the office talking about whether to hang them or shoot them. They were just boys. Not much older than you two..."

Uncle cries as he looks at us: me, Nicola and Bechi who fortunately is a girl and will not have to fight.

"Remo said: 'Let's hang them. To serve as an example for the others we'll hang them in front of the station'. Now there are four boys hanging from the kitchen window. Not the window that overlooks the machine gun. The one on the other side, facing the street. And a sign that reads 'Draft dodgers'. It makes me sick. We just didn't see it coming. We should have reported Remo when he started running the black market out of the signal box. Instead we bought from him."

"Come on Pompeo," says the Turk. "Have a smoke and forget about it." And he gets out a cigarette case that looks like it's made of silver.

"Real cigarettes, French ones, from before the war. I've got one, we'll share it."

"It's your fault too you know, with your cigarettes and your caviar!"

Uncle is shouting now and pushes the Turk away.

"I know how you feel. It's hard for all of us," the Turk says, smiling his half-smile and lighting his half of the cigarette.

Uncle is yelling, swearing. Mother tells us to go outside, but I want to listen. Then we hear shots being fired.

"Someone's shooting."
"Where?"
"Maybe at the bridge?"
"On the other side."
"No, in the village."
"No, at the station."
"What are we going to do?"
We all go outside but we can't work out where the noise is coming from, there are barrages of gunfire and maybe bombs too. But not from planes.
"We'd better take turns staying awake tonight," says the Turk.
It's my turn when I hear someone calling.
"Turk! Turk!" I go to wake him up but he's already at the door with a sickle in his hand.
"Who is it?"
"Friends."
"Who?"
"Sevruga."
"Beluga..."
"Who are you?"
"Girolamo Grandi, now open up for God's sake!"
"Who?"
"The errand boy. Open up!"
The Turk opens the door and it's the errand boy alright, sweaty as ever. Well, it's summer and he's wearing a woolen jacket. With the usual badge on his lapel. No, blow me down! It's not the same one! This one has a hammer and sickle on top of a book. He has a red neckerchief on too. And he's carrying a submachine gun!

"Get inside comrades," he says, dodging the Turk.

"What are you doing?" asks the Turk. All of a sudden there are four armed men in his house.

"Who are you?" he asks.

"Andrea! Enrico!" I exclaim in disbelief.

"You know these people?"

Everyone else has got up from their pallets.

"Yes," I answer. "It's Andrea Cavicchi and his brother..."

"Shut up!" the errand boy says. "No names. "I'm commander Sevruga of the Garibaldi Brigade..."

The Turk laughs out loud, heartily, in spite of the weapons and the circumstances.

"You just can't stop thinking about caviar, can you!" he says.

Uncle swears. "Who are you? And what is this charade?"

"We are freedom fighters," Enrico replies.

"And you've come to fight here?" the Turk asks.

"We've run into a little trouble, you see. We've just sabotaged the railway."

"Not you as well!" Uncle protests.

"Yes, but we were intercepted by the Fascists before we could finish. There was a shoot out and one of our comrades was killed..."

"Someone else from school?" I ask Andrea.

"No, another partisan," he answers.

The errand boy continues: "Now they're looking for us. We need to cross the river and only you can help us, Turk. We're building a new Italy now..."

Then he moves closer to the Turk and says in a low voice: "And when it's all over I'll be the only importer of Volga caviar... Just think, I have it on good authority that Stalin himself likes Imperial Beluga." Then, in a normal voice he goes on: "And we have another problem."

"What?"

"The car."

"What car?"

"My Lancia Ardea, we abandoned it on the embankment."

"You idiots!" explodes the Turk. "Are you trying to get us all shot? We'll have to get rid of it right away. It'll have to be pushed into the river. Then we'll sort out the rest. Pompeo, you guard the house. Use this if need be."

Uncle is left standing there, speechless, with the sickle in his hand. I follow the others.

"Get back into the house," says the Turk, but I decide not to heed him.

"Andrea, what have you done?"

"My name is Nessuno now."

"Come again?"

"Nessuno, like Ulysses. I've made my choice Nello."

"What choice?"

"What side I'm on. It's time for you to choose too..."

I want to say that my choice would be home.

"And what about school?"

"I told you to go back home," growls the Turk, and this time he's not taking no for an answer.

I don't know what they did about the car and getting across the Po. All I know is that it was first light before the Turk came back. And not a moment too soon, because then the Fascists came, led by Remo, armed with machine guns I have never seen on Italian soldiers. But then I think that they're not Italian soldiers, they're Republicans. Even if I don't really know what that means. I know that my father fought in Republican Brigades in Spain. But this lot don't seem to have much in common with "No gods, no masters'. There are all these thoughts going round in my brain when the Germans show up, hot on the heels of the Fascists, with Alsatian dogs straining on leashes. They are doing a search of the whole riverside.

"Come out with your hands up! All of you!" shouts Remo, who is like a different man. Like a werewolf: he's still our signalman, but in the full moon version. This is what pops into my head when I should be concentrating on everything and working things out.

One soldier pulls Mother, another pushes Bechi. I need to stop thinking. I have to defend Bechi, I have to save Mother. Uncle's hair is all standing on end, like he's just got out of bed.

"Remo, what's going on?"

"You tell me! The outlaws' car was seen here, right here! Last night on the embankment! You've turned into Communist filth now, stationmaster indeed!"

Then he points at the Turk: "He knows who commander Sevruga is! He knows because he's a foreigner, a rotten bastard, a devil! Nobody knows who he really is!"

Remo is shouting and yelling, waving his arms about, in a uniform that looks a couple of sizes too big for him. All the riverside people have come out of their huts. The soldiers, the Germans, go inside. My first thought is that they'll find the books, as if having books was a crime. They ask for everyone's papers. Kraus, the German corporal from the station, approaches the Turk, who is the only one not looking at his feet. On the contrary, he actually greets him:

"Good morning."

Kraus is obviously taken aback. He stands there.

"Yah! Good morning to you. So, is it true what zee second lefftenant says, zat you know where zis Serruga eez?"

"Serruga?" The Turk asks.

"Sevruga," Remo corrects him. "You know it's Sevruga, don't think you can fool me!"

"Beluga eez better!" adds another German who has just arrived on the riverside. An officer, judging by his uniform and posture.

"You know Beluga, yah?" he asks the Turk scornfully, in excellent Italian with just a hint of German harshness, better Italian than the fishermen speak in any case.

"It's a cetacean, but also a variety of sturgeon, and a type of caviar, the finest Imperial caviar. This river used to be full of sturgeon, before the war," says the Turk, looking the German officer straight in the eye. I'm watching too now.

"Oberleutnant Mayer," says Remo, under his breath.

"Who?"

"Lieutenant Mayer, the officer in charge of railway defenses."

"I thought you were in charge of defending the homeland?" I say.

He looks away and I take a good look at the lieutenant who is not as young as I think lieutenants usually are. He might be Uncle's age, actually he even looks like him. Now I have no doubts that we Scaramaglis are Aryans, through and through. But suddenly it doesn't matter any more. And I don't understand this choice I have to make. I'm thinking of Cavicchi and all the trouble him, his brother and the errand boy have caused. We're this close to all getting shot. Maybe they'll hang us from the kitchen window of the station too.

"And how would you know about the best caviar?" Lieutenant Mayer asks the Turk sarcastically. But suddenly the Turk's eyes light up. He puts his hand into his pocket and pulls out the mother of pearl spoon:

"Tarabya, 1910, if I remember correctly. You were the orderly of the attaché at the German Embassy. I was the gardener at the Italian ambassador's summer residence. That's where we met..."

"Fogazzaro!" the lieutenant exclaims. "Antonio Fogazzaro!"

We can't believe our eyes when the lieutenant moves towards the Turk and embraces him, I swear, actually embraces him.

"*Piccolo mondo antico*! That was the name of the book! I was studying Italian and you gave me Fogazzaro's book."

I can hear Lieutenant Mayer using the familiar "tu" form of address with the Turk. It's not just a dream.

"White truffles, *francolini* and wine from Ghemme, right?"

"Right! I've been saving a bottle of Ghemme, I'll go and get it... If that's alright?" he says, looking at the Lieutenant.

"Yes, of course, go ahead! I thought you'd be in an embassy somewhere. Or still in Istanbul. What a city!"

We are all speechless. Lieutenant Mayer orders the other soldiers to lower their weapons. Remo protests.

"The Turk is the main suspect in the bombing of the railway. He definitely knows where the rebels are. We need to arrest him now."

"Calm down Second Lieutenant Sacchini. And tell your men to go back to the station."

Remo raises his voice: "I would like to remind you that we are in Republican territory and I am in command!"

The German soldiers put their weapons up again. The Lieutenant looks at him:

"And I would like to remind *you* that if it wasn't for us you and that Mussolini of yours would already be hanging by the neck. Now bugger off! If that is correct Italian," he says, looking in my direction.

I nod and lower my eyes. I look up in time to see Remo ordering his men back up the embankment, while the Lieutenant invites Corporal Kraus to take a seat on the stone bench in front of the house.

"Unfortunately times are hard," says the Turk. "I can't offer you anything to accompany the wine." He fills the glasses with a dark liquid, very different from the Lambrusco that Uncle occasionally drinks. And I wonder just where he was keeping this dusty old bottle. The German soldiers look on from a distance, as the three make a toast. Me, Nicola, Uncle, Mother and Bechi are offered a drink too. The wine is strong and it makes my head spin.

"Life has become so difficult," says the Lieutenant. "It's so hard to understand what our country wants us to do."

Corporal Kraus looks at him: "Yes Hans, I know, but we have to follow orders."

"Just as well, Augustus," he replies.

It's as if the two were friends, not just soldiers together, and they're speaking Italian. I think it's not just so we can understand them, but also so that their men can't. The Turk and the Lieutenant who I now know is called Augustus, have a different kind of sadness in their eyes now. That is what I see.

XLI

"Don't you understand? The Turk saved the lives of everyone here!" Mother says to Quinto, his wife, Mario, Pietro, Toni, Battista, Amelia, Nena, Rita, Maria, Magda, and the rest of the riverside folk who have gathered in front of the Turk's house that evening in the river mist, before the curfew.

"He's in with the Germans! We should burn his house down!" shouts Amelia.

"Yes! We don't want people like that round here!"

"Ask Hitler to come and save you!"

"You, your friend the stationmaster and your whores!" Quinto hollers, gesturing at Mother and Bechi.

"I've always said that nothing good can come of having foreigners here!" Nena from the tavern puts in.

"Drinking wine with the Nazis, indeed! You make me sick!"

"It's disgusting! Wait till Stalin gets here and then you'll see what happens to people like you!"

"You're worse than Remo and his lackeys. At least they've got ideals!"

They don't shout as loud as they'd like to because they're afraid the Germans and the Fascists will come back. And there are spies on the riverside too. Especially now that between the embankment and the river every last shack is inhabited by people's relatives and evacuees from Ferrara, Bologna, and even Rovigo - city people fleeing the air raids. They come here to get the country bombs instead.

Now everyone is anti-Fascist - some are Socialists, some are Communists - but when the partisans came they went straight to the Turk, not to anyone else. I look at these drawn, hungry, angry faces. Mouths with no teeth. Heaps of rags. Arms with stringy tendons in place of muscles that have wasted away for lack of food. Eyes brimming with rage. Fear crawling under their skin. I ask myself whether these are the people my father was fighting for, the people the Cavicchis say they are fighting for. In front of our house, or rather the Turk's house, it's already got to the point of pushing and shoving. Nicola is shielding Mother and Bechi. I join him. They are all mad, but careful not to make too much noise.

We need to take a stand, one gun shot would be enough. They'd all scarper. Lieutenant Mayer, Augustus, would send soldiers to save us. But if the Germans came to save us then all these angry people here would be right. I don't know. I don't know what to do. I'm standing in front of Mother but she tells me to move out of the way, to go away. And I think they're going to drown us all in the river. Or attack us with pitchforks. The Fascists, Remo in first place, would be glad. Then I think about how stupid I was that day in Ferrara, with Cavicchi's father. I met a person who fought side by side with my father and all I could do was ask idiotic questions and worry about getting home. I cried. I complained about my surname. But I didn't ask him anything. No gods, no masters... What does it mean? That's what I should have asked him.

The Turk is speaking but I'm not listening to him. I think we're all going to die, that this is it. At the hands of these people, I think. When I think of all the things the Turk has done for them, for us, for everyone... He, on the other hand, is unflappable. He's standing in front of Uncle and looking at that rabble, emotionless apart from that mocking half smile of his.

"Calm down! Let them through!" Nena orders softly.

The tension melts away, replaced by fear. Who's coming? Gatherings are prohibited. If it's the Germans coming back... But it's commander Sevruga, with a gang of boys. I look but the Cavicchis aren't with them. Many of them have red neckerchiefs on, and all of them are armed.

"You'd be better off taking care of the spies on the riverside," says commander Sevruga sternly, looking over the top of his glasses. He's sweating again, but like a man, not a flustered errand boy. "The Turk is under our protection."

"You have nothing to fear," he says to the Turk.

The Turk looks at him, like he's wondering what he's doing on this side of the river. I don't know what protection he means, seeing as the Fascists and the Germans are in command.

"We don't have control of the riverside," says Commander Sevruga. "But our men are everywhere and the Turk must not be harmed. Is that clear?"

Some nod, looking convinced. That's one way of telling the Socialists and Communists apart from the others, because they agree with Commander Sevruga, formerly the errand boy. Then Commander Sevruga comes over to us and says to the Turk:

"Now we're quits, but it would be better if you went away for a while. You're not safe here."

"The only way I'm leaving here is in a wooden box," says the Turk, in a voice that brooks no argument. "You can't understand, Commander Sevruga."

He actually calls him Commander. The errand boy! Quinto, Mario and the others are heading off, back to their huts. When there are partisans around people are afraid, it takes nothing to be shot as a traitor, or get your house burned down. I look at one of the errand boy's soldiers. He's wearing short trousers, a red neckerchief and boots. He's got the look of the troublemaker about him and no mistake. He's smoking. I don't think he's much older than me. He has a military shirt on and a bandolier full of magazines for the machine gun slung over his shoulder. The Turk looks at the errand boy and says:

"I made my choice, years ago. No gods, no masters... I've served all kinds of lords and masters and I could have had an easier life too."

"As a cosmopolitan?"

"As a cosmopolitan, if you like. But I soon saw that all masters screw you over in the end, and the only way not to be taken for a fool is to be your own boss. Or go back to where you belong. And this river, the Po River, is where I belong."

It sounds like a confession given to a priest but it's not. It's delivered eye to eye, in the fog, one autumn evening of 1944. It's the first time I've heard the Turk string so many words together, and it's so private, so personal, that I am shocked. The errand boy is listening and maybe this time he's getting it. And even if he hasn't got the message, there's a voice in his head telling him that the Turk is telling the truth, a deeper truth. There's the same voice in my head. And that phrase: no gods, no masters.

"As you wish," says commander Sevruga. "But it's not safe here. And we have had orders to fall back towards the Apennines. That's if we can get through the German lines. And the front is moving north. There will be more bombings. The river, your river," he emphasises, looking at the Turk, "is too strategic a transport route to leave in enemy hands."

"Goodnight."

"Goodnight."

The errand boy gives a sign and his men follow him. He's a leader now. Maybe he always has been, and we just didn't see it. Before I go to bed Uncle says that I can forget about school this year. There are no passenger trains, so there's no way to get to Ferrara. My only consolation is that Cavicchi will miss a year too. Perhaps we all will. Maybe we'll all be dead before the trains start running again. If they ever do.

There's no radio on the riverside, because there's no electricity. Nena who comes to apologize to the Turk because she didn't know he had links with the party, as in the Communist party, not the Fascist Party this time, tells us that the Allies, which is what we now call the American and British forces, have taken Rimini and crossed the Gothic line. Nena says that the enemy's days are numbered. I feel like asking her who the enemy is, but just out of mischief. Of course I know she's talking about the Germans.

XLII

When we go into the woods we take care not to run into any Germans. Or partisans. Or Fascists, because that's what we call the soldiers of the Republic now. The homeland can take a running jump as far as I'm concerned. The Turk tells us to keep together, me and Nicola, and never to separate, to say that we're woodcutters and to always carry a billhook. We have papers to show if we get stopped. It's important to have them because the conscription age has been lowered and we have to be able to prove that we're too young.

Mother and Bechi are better off not going out at all, and spend their days cleaning, sweeping, mending, reading. At least they get to read all those books in Bechi's trunk. They would cook too, if there was something to cook, but we're always short of something. Even Pasquina in the signal box doesn't have much in stock these days. Not even if you pay through the nose. The Turk does odd jobs and stays near the house. Only Uncle still goes to the station every day to do his shifts. On my bicycle and wearing his helmet. Every evening he tells us how little is left of his railway. He keeps a record of the bombings, the damage, engines that are out of action, lost carriages and smashed wagons. And the people who've died, but he's less interested in them. He takes the German engineers to the places where sleepers and rails need changing. He lives in a different world to us, and when he tells us about it in the evening it seems so far away. But that world used to be our world too.

Me and Nicola spend the days picking mushrooms and herbs, gathering wood to burn and going hunting and fishing. But the river is not generous, the woods are stripped bare and fights break out over firewood. Everyone else is out looking for plants and roots to eat too. On the riverside, our riverside, there are dozens, perhaps hundreds of new people, evacuees. All in the same place. One time we almost come to blows with Mario over a log full of *piopparelli* mushrooms.

"Let's go halfers," says Nicola. "Isn't your father a Communist?"

Mario looks at him and replies: "Yes but he's the secretary of the cell."

"Of the what?" I ask.

"Oh wake up Nellino! This lot are just like the Fascists, wanting to lord it over everyone," says Nicola.

"What? You calling my father a Fascist?"

"Well, what was he up till yesterday?"

"And your uncle was a master."

"And your father was a fish thief."

"A what?"

"A fish thief. Everyone knows that the Turk took all the sturgeons and put a spell on them. And the priest with his church songs..."

"The priest doesn't even fish any more."

"'Cos there aren't any fish left."

"A bit like your father used to say," Nicola says to me.

"My father?" I ask, amazed, because the only person who ever talks about him is Uncle.

"Yeah, and my father said it too, that day with the errand boy."

"What was that?"

"No gods no sturgeons..."

I'm about to correct him but instead I burst out laughing: "Yeah! No gods, no sturgeons..."

Mario doesn't understand what we're talking about but slyly nabs the mushrooms and hurries off home.

Winter is drawing near. As well as not having much wood or coal, we don't have much in the way of warm clothes either. I've got a lot taller and I have to wear Uncle's clothes. But Uncle doesn't have many clothes because he wears his railway uniform. Just as well that the biggest mirror in the Turk's house is hardly big enough to shave in front of. The advance of the Allies, which was supposed to be imminent in September, proves to be much slower than the onward march of the cold weather. The winter has a knack for being imminent. On December 20th the British are in Faenza, according to the radio. Nena is the only one who listens to it these days because Uncle can't tune in to Radio Londra in the station.

"Where's that?"

"In Romagna."

"Near here then."

"I think Christmas will get here first," says Uncle who has got so thin that he has to keep adding holes to his belt to keep up his trousers, which look looser and more threadbare every day. Even the Turk, who used to be a big man, is starting to lose muscle. I see these things because us men get dressed together in the morning, while the women are heating up the water in the kitchen. We have hot water for breakfast, with herbs. Now and again Uncle manages to get some milk from Pasquina. As for coffee, no chance. Then it's the women's turn to get dressed, and we're not allowed into the bedroom. Mother and Bechi take ages to do their hair.

"We mustn't let standards slip," Mother always says, and Bechi nods in agreement. She hardly ever speaks now. There's nothing to say. We are prisoners on the riverside. The Fascists have taken all the remaining bicycles. The country needs them, Remo says. And he issues us an official Social Republic receipt for them. Uncle walks to the station now. It takes almost an hour, more if it's raining.

XLIII

With the blessing of Don Antonio, Mother decides that the birth of Our Lord is a more important festivity than St. Nicholas. So the proper celebrations will be on December 25th. Mother says that everyone celebrates on that day, all round the world. The Turk comments that Saint Nicholas isn't doing badly for himself either. To tell the truth I don't mind, because Saint Nicholas is of course Nicola's saint's day too, his personal celebration. At Christmas, on the other hand, we're all equal. "Like we have something to celebrate," grumbles Uncle.

During the month of December the Fascists and the Germans commandeer everything they can get their hands on, here on the riverside, and beyond. They even take three pigs that belong to the butcher who usually supplies Remo under the counter for the black market. Everyone gets an official receipt, of course.

"Just as well the partisans have retreated into the mountains and don't have to eat here too," Nena says one day. She's a regular round at our house now. She brings us the news and stops for a chat. No-one goes to the tavern these days. Wine is in short supply, and it's pretty rough anyway. The tavern is not in a good position because it's near the bridge that was bombed into heaps of sunken wreckage. The Germans have tried twice to construct a new pontoon bridge near the old one, on the bigger boats. There's bombing every day now. Luckily from high up, because if they fired at close range there would be nothing left standing round here. Now beside the ramshackle bridge there are military craft that the German sappers use to take supplies across, and are careful to keep out of sight from the Americans. There's even a sort of collapsible ferry. But Nena's tavern is by the bridge and that's enough to make no-one want to go there any more. Apart from the soldiers who Nena serves against her will. She shuts up shop as soon as she can. And when she does she comes to ours.

Mother says we can't go on like this for much longer. Uncle and Bechi are both locked in silence. Neither of them says a word any more. Nicola is convinced that by Christmas his saint, Saint Nicholas, will rustle up a feast worthy of the name, so every day he goes down to the river, which is shrouded in fog. He puts down fishing lines with hooks, but it's so cold we have trouble finding worms to put on them. There's nothing here now.

The odd bits and pieces we manage to get with our ration cards are not enough for our everyday meals, let alone Christmas. On the black market everything costs too much and even there, there's not much to be had these days. The only things moving on the railway are military trains, carrying weapons, ammunition, fuel. One of these December days Uncle arrives home even paler than usual, and after not saying a word for hours, tells us about a train that was diverted through Ferrara. It was supposed to go north but it got sent here instead.

"The transit order was marked confidential as usual," Uncle says. "When it arrived in the station I had a look at it and it looked like those cattle wagons that they used to transport cows in, from the fields to the dairy. When it stopped to take on water for the locomotive, I could hear bleating coming from inside the wagons, like sheep, or lambs – to feed the German troops. There goes our Christmas lunch, I thought."

"The train was guarded but you could hear the noises just the same. Luckily the alarm went off before the planes showed up. Not the usual big bombers, but fighter planes, I don't know what they were... They started shooting at the station..." Uncle is lost for words again.

"What did you do?" Mother asks.

Silence.

"What happened?"

"Well, the Germans guarding the convoy lay down on the ground."

"And what about you?"

"I was going to try and get my hands on a lamb when the door of one of the wagons opened and they all ran out."

"All what? The lambs?"

"No! It was a woman, with two children, then another boy. They all started running towards Remo's signal box. There were people on the train, don't you see, Argia? The noises I heard were people crying inside those cattle wagons..."

"But what happened?"

"The Germans started shouting: 'Halt! Halt! Achtung!' Or whatever it is they say... Remo came out of the signal box and fired a shot in the air. At least I think he fired it in the air. They all stopped, all except the little boy who just kept on running. Remo shouted: 'Stop, you little idiot!' But the boy just kept running, he didn't understand, maybe he didn't hear him. Corporal Kraus shouted: 'Get him!'. He shouted it in Italian to the soldiers in the National Guard, Remo's men, and they all started running. Then I heard the shot."

"What shot?"

"It was one of the anti-aircraft gunners, the ones who drink our coffee. He was crowing: 'Got him!' 'I got him!' Not even Remo, not even Corporal Kraus had the courage to look at the soldier who fired the shot. He was cheering like he was at the shooting range. The boy's mother started screaming, but the Germans got hold of her and pushed her back into the cattle wagon. She was screaming her head off but all the others were just wailing quietly like before. Remo turned round to me and said: 'Jews.' That's all he said. Not another word. Not another look, then the train set off again."

Uncle says it doesn't matter if there's no food. At Christmas Mother manages to make a broth out of pumpkin, with song birds in it that me and Nicola have trapped. She gets some rice on the black market and puts that in too. We nibble on the birds and the boiled pumpkin. The Turk roasts a couple of chubs that Nicola has fished, that are more bones than meat.

"Better that way," says Mother. "If things take longer to eat in the end you feel fuller."

I think of the lamb we missed out on. I have to admit that I think more about the lamb than the boy Uncle told us about.

The New Year starts with bombs. The errand boy, or rather Commander Sevruga, was right: it is only going to get worse here by the Po. Mother still does Bechi's hair every day but she doesn't put hers up any more, she can't be bothered. The bombing continues for the whole of January, and the riverside huts get bombed for the first time, a sign that they're just dropping them at random, anywhere around the river. Some of the shacks are destroyed and the evacuees are the first to get moved on again. No-one really goes anywhere these days, because of who you might meet, or the risk of getting hit by a bomb, or mowed down by a machine gun, or picked up by a German patrol and not showing your papers in time. We are all paralyzed. Not even books can keep us together. Only Bechi still devours them one after another, but in total silence.

"We have to do something," Mother repeats incessantly.

The Turk and Uncle don't even bother answering. It's cold, so cold that we pile on all the raggedy old clothes we can find. There are no more trees to burn, and the damp fog sneaks into every nook and cranny. Even the straw pallets are damp. Our clothes stink and there's no point in washing them because they would never dry out.

When I read *The Paul Street Boys* for the umpteenth time, because it's the only book that seems to suit all this gloom and doom, I feel just like Nemecsek with his fever, about to die. Then I think of the Trojan war that lasted ten years and I calculate that if this war is the same we're about half way through. How on earth are we going to survive for the rest of it?

I hear Mother telling Uncle: "Can't you see he's burning up? It's not quinine we need. We need heat, blankets, a proper house!"

"And where am I supposed to get blankets and a proper house?" Uncle replies wearily.

"I think we should go back to the station. Please Pompeo." Mother is irresistible when she smiles. I know even if I can't see her.

"But what about the bombs? And the Germans?"

"I'd rather live with bombs than all this damp. These people live like savages!" Mother howls.

"We live as best we can," the Turk says apologetically. But he's tired of Mother's constant state of agitation too.

We are going to move back to the station. Uncle invites the Turk and his family to come with us but the Turk just says: "This is my home."

Then he looks at Nicola and Bechi and says: "This is our home."

By the end of January we are in the station again. Or rather what's left of the station. On Remo's signal box someone has painted the words "HONOR LOYALTY COURAGE' in big letters. Half of the flat, our half, needs straightening up a bit, but luckily no-one's been in it while we've been away. Apart from bombs and bullets. My bed is still there, the cupboards have the same smells in them, the marble table stands in the kitchen. It's cold, of course, but not damp like the Turk's house.

"Well, if we need to we can always burn some of the furniture," Mother suggests, before she sees the look of horror on Uncle's face.

"Go on, for Nellino..."

He's still horrified. I think that we'll probably get killed by a bomb sooner or later, but at least we'll be comfortable. The railway is unusable, even for the Germans. The train carrying the Jews was the last one that got through. The sappers can't patch up all the missing stretches of track. The National Republican Railway Guard, which is what the Railway Militia Corps is called now, are based in the station, but if there are no searches to do they play cards. Sometimes Uncle joins them when he's not out and about taking stock of all the damage. When the alarm goes off we go down into the basement and the gunners go up onto the terrace. They aim for the planes overhead, which are always out of their reach, and which are targeting the Po. Because the railway line has been blown to smithereens.

Slowly, I recover. Pasquina, who is glad to have a female neighbor again and not just military, gives us an egg or some black bread every so often. War is such an everyday fact of life now that it's like we've always lived this way. I wonder about Cavicchi, or rather the Cavicchi brothers, and the errand boy. Maybe I should be doing something for the cause too.

"Study," Uncle is always telling me. As if it were easy to study in these conditions.

"Leave him in peace Pompeo."

"He has to earn his keep too, you know"

"With what we've got to give him..."

In the evening we listen to Radio Londra and nobody says a word. Littorio and Benito, Remo's twins, have told me that their father listens to it too. Now that there are no trains the Germans are not guarding the station any more, just the Fascists.

XLIV

One day Uncle observes that it's almost sturgeon season. I don't want to think about the state of the riverbed these days, and all the dead bodies, bombs, wreckage and scrap metal that have been washed up onto the banks. I don't even have my bicycle to go and take a look. No-one knows whether the spring will bring sturgeons, but people are saying that the partisans are on their way back. In the sense that there is news of attacks, shootings, people getting killed. It is also rumored that somewhere they set fire to the conscription lists to stop more boys getting called up. On Radio Londra there's news of fighting on all possible fronts, but here in Italy the war is playing cards. And we are prisoners in the game.

Then all of a sudden everything changes. It's April and every day there are compact formations of hulking great planes heading for the Po. The air is filled with the constant roar of engines. Propellers. Explosions. I wonder what the errand boy would make of it all. Not the Commander Sevruga we know now, but the pudgy errand boy of the past who loved Marinetti. He would certainly have got his fill of progress and modernity, engines and noise. Every day Radio Londra says that the Allies are advancing. Gaining ground, taking new cities. You wouldn't know it here. Uncle, who has a good grasp of geography, says that it's true, that it's really just a matter of days. The English, or rather the British, are in Alfonsine, which is on the other side of Ravenna.

"Maybe we should do something for the cause too," Uncle says to Mother.

"But what?" I ask.

"Not you. Us as in your Mother and I. You're too young."

"What about Cavicchi then?"

"Don't say that name! Do you want to get him killed? Careless talk costs lives!"

"Sorry."

"Sorry won't help your friend."

"Let's just give it time, Pompeo," says Mother.

"We can't wait forever, you know. We're overrun with Fascists here."

"We could cut their throats," I suggest.

"Now you're just being stupid," says Uncle witheringly.

We wait. But we don't need to wait long because suddenly it's like the end of the world is starting. The German sappers put in an appearance, but only to blow up the iron bridge that wasn't taken out by the bombs. Troops come past the station on all modes of transport imaginable: trucks, cars, motorcycles, even horses and mules. They're heading for the Po. We see Remo loading up a car. I snidely wonder whether he's requisitioned it and left a receipt. I've learned to be suspicious now. Remo, the twins and Pasquina are in the car, and the gunners and all the members of the Railway Militia or whatever they're called are hanging onto the outside of it for dear life. Others are taking out bicycles, our bicycles, and there are four people balanced on one motorcycle. Everyone's bailing out, and in a hurry.

"Blast them all to buggery!" curses Uncle, at the people and vehicles streaming quietly past the station.

In the sky propellers throb. Then silence, a deathly hush. I mean you can still hear explosions in the distance, and shooting, lots of shooting. But it's like the station is floating on a cloud. There's no-one around, they've all gone. The machine gun is still on the terrace, but in pieces. The soldiers smashed it up before they left. All around us is the desolate sight of a war that lasted half that of the Trojan war, but had no hero. Honor, loyalty, courage, I think. The words are still written on the wall of the signal box.

"Do you think this means the war is over?" I ask Uncle.

He looks at me: "Who knows?"

We don't know what's going on. There's nobody else here. We stand there in front of the station, not on the train side but on the road side, like lost souls. We get found by two jeeps that arrive bearing soldiers wearing helmets that look like bowls. They don't even look like they're worried someone might shoot at them. When they reach us Uncle and I raise our hands, as if we were the ones losing the war.

"*Tu Mussolini*?" one of the soldiers asks me, laughing.

I shake my head.

"Good lad!"

And he tosses me a pack of cigarettes. A whole pack! I scrabble for it. A minute later the soldiers are inside the station.

"Where are you from? American? English?" Uncle asks.

Finally he's getting a chance to show off his English, which doesn't sound all that great to me. "New Zealand," one of the soldiers answers, "*Nuova Zelanda*."

His Italian sounds a lot better than Uncle's English.

Other trucks pull up with more soldiers from the same place, which I know I couldn't find on a map.

"I think it's near Australia," Uncle tells me, but even he doesn't sound too sure.

"Can we set up a garrison in this station?" asks one, who looks like an NCO.

They're asking for permission? Not even our own army has ever asked for permission.

"At your service," replies Uncle.

In an hour, maybe less, the downstairs offices are occupied. Mother has found some coffee in the hastily abandoned signal box, but they have tea, condensed milk, and, best of all, chocolate. We are their guests, in other words. They stay long enough to occupy the village and the surrounding area, and to check that the railway is out of action.

"We hit this area hard, no doubt about it," says the NCO to Uncle.

Then they take everything away because they've set up camp down by the embankment. They tell us that by tomorrow the English and probably the Americans will be here too. They seem happy to keep us informed, so I ask:

"And the Germans?"

"Down there," he replies, pointing towards the Po and the riverside.

That night, for the first time in years, there are no soldiers around. Not the new ones or the old ones. In the morning there is a constant procession of trucks, tanks and jeeps, with and without machine guns, armored vehicles and strange contraptions that Uncle tells me are called amphibians. And soldiers in different uniforms, with different helmets, even of different races. "There are black people too," I tell Uncle.

He laughs: "Well, we've got Turks!"

I think about the Turk, and the riverside. Here it's easy to feel like the war is over, but maybe things are different down there.

"Can I go down?" I ask Uncle.

"Yes, but just make sure you come back in one piece. Argia would never forgive me if anything happened to you."

"Are you worried about Nicola and Bechi too?" I ask.

"Yes," says Uncle. "Be sure you're home before nightfall."

I think he meant, be sure to get back alive. When I arrive at the riverside I realise I have never seen war so close up before. In the sense that everyone is fighting but no-one really knows who or where the enemy is. There's gunfire on the embankment. Obviously there are still Germans by the river, maybe Fascists too. But they are spread out, gathered in little groups near the bridges, or what's left of them. I take the safest path to the Turk's house, passing among the New Zealand soldiers who are advancing calmly and don't even notice me coming through on foot.

If anyone stops me, they ask: "*Tu Mussolini*?"

When I shake my head they give me a piece of chocolate or a packet of cigarettes.

I get to the Turk's house and knock on the door.

The Turk says: "Come in, you're welcome here!"

"What did you say?" I ask.

"Ah, it's you Nellino! Forgive me, I thought it was more New Zealand soldiers."

"There's been a lot going on these last few days," Nicola says. "Even Lieutenant Mayer came by on his motorcycle to say goodbye. To hell with him, I say..."

"Nicola!" the Turk scolds him.

"He was a Nazi, father..."

"But a good person too, Nicola."

I make out Bechi in the gloom of the kitchen.

"Hi Bechi."

She gives me a little wave.

"She's still not talking, then?"

The Turk shakes his head.

Nicola continues excitedly: "They're dropping like flies now, those bastards. Some are surrendering, others are trying to escape. Yesterday there were even German tanks, right here, but the others forced them into the river. You should have seen it, they were drowning like rats right in front of my eyes. I've been going to the bridge for the last three days, they're trying anything to get across. I even saw Remo with money in his hand, big five hundred lire banknotes, trying to buy one of the sunken boats. Then he went west, they say there are other bridges still standing."

"Yeah right," I say. "Like we haven't seen all the planes bombing the Po. There's no way there are any bridges left."

"Worse for Remo," Nicola continues. "You should have seen the Germans! They were going crazy, driving their cars into the river."

"The Americans have got trucks that go in the water," I interrupt. "They passed by the station today."

"But how do they go in the water?"

"They're like a cross between a truck and a boat... That's how they won you know. It's a question of military supremacy."

"No," says the Turk. "They won because they have food and cigarettes." He has a packet of biscuits in one hand and a lit cigarette in the other and a smile on his face that I haven't seen since the sturgeon days.

Nicola is on a roll: "Y'know, the Germans came to the riverside and took wash tubs, and two wine barrels from Nena's and went into the river with them to try and swim across. They're all waiting at the river crossings, looking for a way to get over. If they don't make it they surrender. Or drown. Or..."

"Or what?"

Nicola makes a knowing expression: "Or they get shot by the partisans, people from round here, who hide behind the trees on the river bank and 'Bang! Bang!' There's not one German or Fascist who gets through alive... The Allies take them away with their arms up in the air, but the partisans don't let any of them leave under their own steam..."

Nicola pauses for breath then says: "And they're right, these bastards deserve everything that's coming to them."

"We should have done something about it before now," I say.

I feel a bit guilty, what with Cavicchi being a partisan and all.

The Turk intervenes in the ensuing silence: "You can tell your Uncle that everything's okay down here. I've heard that the Allies are going to cross the river tomorrow. Then it'll really be over."

With that, he gives me a slap on the back and sends me home. He knows that Mother worries. I say goodbye and head back to the station.

XLV

Now, there's nothing left of the Turk I know, have always known. The Turk before me is a man without a face, hands trembling, bewildered, covered in blood, kneeling on the river sand. He's holding Nicola in his arms and in the boat there is a huge white sturgeon, bigger than anything I've ever seen before. The Turk is biting on his lip and shouting and crying, incoherent. Then someone understands what he's saying and shouts:

"Get a doctor! Get a doctor for God's sake!"

"A doctor? Where on earth are we going to find a doctor?"

"It doesn't matter! Just get one!"

"Ask the Allies, they'll have a doctor!"

The other people from the riverside are coming down now. Someone has told Uncle who gets here with Mother... Bechi is probably here too but I can't see her.

I'd gone down to the river because I wanted to see for myself what Nicola told me yesterday. I wanted to see the end of the war, I wanted to be there. I'd come to wake Nicola up. But he was already awake. Then.

"We don't need a doctor, we don't need anything," says the Turk in a muffled voice, spitting out tears, sniffing and clinging tight to that body that looks like an empty sack, with the strength he uses to bring in a sturgeon. We all look at Nicola and there is a trickle of blood coming out of his mouth. His eyes are rolled back in his head and his skin is pale, as if from the cold, but it's different to that.

"He's dead, dead, dead..."

The Turk wails and doesn't even have the strength to open his eyes, and doesn't know what to do with those big hands of his that are holding onto Nicola for dear life, but are no use, no use any more.

"How could it have happened?"

"The war's over!"

"Yeah the Germans have done a runner!"

"Scum of the earth!"

"Remo's gone too."

"With that harpy Pasquina and those bastard twins of his!"

"I hope they drown in the Po! I hope they all drown in the Po!"

"But what were you doing out on the river, Turk?"

"Where did you get the boat?"

"Friends with the Germans, are you?"

"Were you taking them across the river?"

"You been double dealing, Turk?"

The fishermen have all come along. The children from the village. Everyone.

"This happening, now that the war is over!" they keep saying. "Now that the New Zealanders are here."

"And the Americans."

"And the partisans."

"Someone should go and find out, find someone in command."

"But this is war business."

"No, this is fishy business, that's what it is."

"We were out on the Po, last night, in the boat."

I look at the Turk but he does not look up. He looks like Michelangelo's statue, the *Pietà*, but it's not the Madonna he's holding in his arms. The arms holding Nicola are great strong arms, arms that can hold up the world, or pull in a hundred kilo sturgeon, like the one in the boat. Everyone's looking at the fish now.

"But it's white!" someone says. "It's huge!"

"What were they thinking of, going fishing when there's a war on?"

"But the war's finished now."

"Yeah, and we saw how that turned out."

"Look at his boy."

"They were still shooting last night."

"But the Germans surrendered yesterday..."

"No, they didn't surrender..."

"But they're running away, the war is over."

The Turk doesn't hear a word of it. I can see that. I just can't bring myself to look at Nicola.

"What were you doing out here at dawn?"

The Turk tries to take a breath, to stop his tears and regain his dignity. He looks over at the sturgeon: "That's his, that's Nicola's fish. He's the one who dreamt it."

Then he kisses Nicola's head, his hair that is all matted with blood. And holds him tighter. I feel like I'm going to cry but then I see Bechi, who's figured it out, and she screams and throws herself on the ground, her face in the Po sand. Mother comes over to her, she hugs her tight, and pulls her to her feet.

The other women join them. It's like there has been another war here.

I see Uncle approach the Turk, and clasp his arm. I join him. He looks at me but it's like he's looking straight through me.

"I said we weren't going to go out but he wouldn't take no for an answer. Kept on saying that he'd dreamt about it, that he'd seen it."

"But what happened?" Uncle asks.

The Turk takes a deep breath before replying: "It was almost dawn and we hadn't really slept because there was a lot of shooting during the night. Then it all went quiet and I fell asleep. I only woke up when I heard someone calling my name. It was Nicola..."

But just saying Nicola's name makes him crumple up, and his eyes fill with tears again.

"Arturo!" Uncle says his name firmly: "Arturo!"

Till then I'd never known that the Turk had a name and that someone knew it. Uncle! Uncle knew the Turk's name was Arturo.

"Nicola told me he'd had the dream."

"What dream?"

"The dream about the sturgeon."

"No way," I said. "No-one's been fishing for years!"

The Turk continues: "He said: 'Father, I dreamt it, I really did. There was a white horse running towards me and as it got closer it turned into a huge sturgeon.' I asked him: 'Then what happened?' and he said: 'Then the train passed through'. 'Come again?' I said. He said that after the sturgeon the train came through. I said that he wasn't well, that he had a fever.

But he said he'd dreamt it for real, that we had to go down to the river. I kept saying that there was a war on, that they were still shooting. He was insisting that the war was finished, that the Germans had fled, it had been on the radio, he said. I said that we'd no nets, no boat, but he insisted that everything was ready, where we'd hidden it. And it was true. Everything was in good nick, kept well out of sight of everyone round here, and the Germans."

"But where?"

"Here, for the love of God, it was all here, hidden in the reeds on the island. If only this damned war had sunk our boat too Nicola would still be alive."

The Turk looks at me then and says: "You were right... You were all right... I should have kept him at school with Nellino."

Uncle is impatient. He wants to know what happened, before the soldiers turn up, the partisans, the New Zealanders, the Americans, before the news makes it to the village...

"Then what happened?" Uncle sounds very authoritative, I've never heard him use that tone of voice before. Gentle but firm, like he's giving orders but at the same time understands the Turk's pain. I'm impressed. The Turk calms down, and speaks through his tears.

"So we went out on the river. Not far from where the boat was hidden and you could see the anti-aircraft tracers on the other side of the river, the lights and the flares, the shooting. With every flash of light you could see the Germans running along the river bank. I told Nicola to look, to see that the war was still going on, but he said no, that the Germans were running for their lives, that the war was over, that Nena heard it on the radio. But I kept a look out," continues the Turk, "and

I could see it was war. Then Nicola said there was something in the net, pulling the net out of his hands. 'Father help me,' he said. 'It's a whopper'. It was huge, I've never felt anything thrashing so hard. The current was taking us downstream and the net with the sturgeon was behind us, holding us like a mooring post. I thought he'd netted a German tank! But he could feel it pulling. He said: 'See? I told you I'd had the dream. The dream never fails'. I was worried it might break the net, or that even if we brought it in we might not manage to sell it. But he said: 'The war's finished. People will want to celebrate, and if not we'll eat it ourselves, like that time with the Lady's caviar. Don't you remember?' How could I forget? It was a dinner worth more than the last supper to me. When it came under the boat everything went quiet. I'd never seen a fish that big... I said to Nicola: 'Not even in Astrakhan...'"

The Turk starts crying again, thickly. His lip is bleeding because he's biting down on it to try and stop the tears, and he's digging his fingers into Nicola's clothes, like he's trying to hold onto the memories. His voice cracks, but Uncle wants to know more. He wants to know what happened before the news gets out, before someone gets the idea that the Turk was taking the Germans across the river.

"It was enormous, a massive fish. Look, it's in the boat."

And he points to the boat pulled up on the sand, with the huge fish lying in it, a trickle of blood running down between the bony plates on its sides. A rivulet of blood from its head. Just like Nicola. But one is a fish. And the other is a boy.

I can feel my tears welling up, but then Uncle puts his arm round me too and says: "You listen too, another witness could come in handy."

"We harpooned the sturgeon, twice to make sure it wouldn't turn the boat over, or break the net, or tip us into the river. Then we started pulling it to the boat, little by little, and we hit it again. We tied a rope around it and tried to haul it up with the gaff. It was almost impossible, but we knew we couldn't keep it alive. Or keep it in the water. We had to get it into the boat, so we came into this creek near the woods. The sun was coming up by this time and the water is slower here, so we managed to pull it up more easily. Everything was covered in blood, including the net. Nicola said he'd never seen a white one before. Neither had I. Father and son we were..."

At that the Turk starts crying again but Uncle doesn't let up. He asks him more about it, forces him to keep speaking. There are other people coming down now, we have to know.

"What's it to you anyway Pompeo?" says the Turk, addressing him with the familiar "tu" for the very first time.

"Just tell me! Tell me what happened!"

"We pulled up the fish, and the net. In the old days the kids would have been running home shouting 'A whopper!' 'A whopper!' Do you remember?"

"Yes, I remember it well... But what happened next?"

"I heard a shot being fired. So I turned to Nicola to say 'See? The war isn't exactly finished, maybe we should get back home to Bechi...' But as I was turning round I heard a cry here, in the boat, and it wasn't the sturgeon. Nicola fell forward. 'Stop fooling around,' I said to him. 'You'll give your old man a heart attack!' But already he had the look of death on him. 'Nicola, what's wrong?' I asked him, but he didn't answer me. The blood started coming. At first I thought it was from the sturgeon, but then I saw it was coming through Nicola's jacket. He didn't speak, and there was blood coming out of his mouth too. So I started to row back to shore, screaming for someone to help me. But there are no boats in the Po these days, the Germans have taken them all. I just kept rowing and shouting for help till I got here. When we reached the bank I felt for his pulse and I looked into his eyes and I just knew. Those bastards! Those bastards killed my son!"

The Turk pulls Nicola to him like he'll never ever leave him. And we still can't understand it. Why they went fishing. How it all ended like that. Then Uncle gets to his feet and offers me an American cigarette. The war really is over. Nicola was right.

Bechi left after the funeral. I never went back to the riverside again.

EPILOGUE

The world has changed since then but I still like traveling by train. And that's how I came to Italy on Christmas Day. A quick visit to Venice on the way, like a normal tourist. Then Ferrara. How small it seems to me now: when I was at school it seemed so big... The taxi from the station to the hotel cost me three euros, hardly worth it.

This is my first visit to Italy in a very long time. I only decided to come because since Rebecca died there's not much point to life any more. I've tried to keep going, of course. One day she just went. Died, I mean. I don't even know how to put it into words, how to convince myself that she's really gone. After a lifetime together it is so very painful. One day in front of the mirror I gave myself a stern talking to: "Nello, you're not yet eighty. You're a good-looking fellow, healthy. Life goes on. Get off your backside, and do something."

And I've tried, I really have, but when you're on your own, the things you used to like just don't hold the same appeal any more. That's when I started to have a feeling I'd never had before: for the first time in my life I felt homesick, I felt the pull of the places of my childhood, the past I thought I had buried forever. But you can't just wish things away. You can flutter around like a butterfly your whole life but then something or someone catches up with you. You can't escape your destiny.

The day I understood that, I was at a party, the usual boring fundraisers where all the do-gooders gather to smile at each other. They were raising money to save a villa in Tarabya, the old summer residence of the Italian ambassador in Istanbul. Some Italians had come along to support the cause too, as if theirs was the only run-down villa on the Bosphorus, as if it wasn't obvious that together with these wooden houses we are losing a piece of history that has been around a lot longer than we have. And for the first time I got to thinking of the Turk, down on the riverside when I was a boy, who had been a gardener in that villa. And Nicola, whose memory I had buried. It was by chance that I found myself in Turkey: fate had taken me by the shirt.

So after that I decided to come back to Italy. For Christmas. Now I'm all alone in the world I have no-one to celebrate with anyway. We had a son, Rebecca and I – Andrea is his name – but we've not spoken in years. The last time we saw each other was at Rebecca's funeral, and then it was just a quick hug, a few words, before we went our separate ways. Or rather he did. Andrea lives here in Italy, actually. Every now and then he sends me an email, but I don't read them any more. Those contraptions, computers, are just too difficult for me. There's a limit to this constant pursuit of progress, and it's the years passing that is my limit. But I realize now that even though I gave him my surname and everything else, I don't think I've been a better father to him than mine was to me. Or maybe it's just the case that you don't need a father to grow up, to live your life.

I was at university when I met up with Rebecca again - that was Bechi's full name: Rebecca Macchioro, the Jewish niece not of the Turk but of the caviar lady. Whose name was Clara Macchioro. Bechi, as we all realized back then, was something special. One smart cookie she was. I couldn't believe it when I heard that after the war she'd done all her school exams in two years. That's what all the books in the trunk were for.

Well, I don't want to waffle on. Rebecca and I got married. Yes, married. And we spent the rest of the twentieth century together, selling caviar. That's how it went – I became a cosmopolitan, as we would have said back in the day – that strange word the errand boy introduced which became common usage for us. A life devoted to caviar, the river's legacy, if you like: Beluga, Sevruga, Asetra, Asetra garabrum... Iran under the Shah, Switzerland, Turkey, the former Soviet Union, and the countries that emerged after the fall of Communism. Over the years we watched the world order break down and put itself back together, with a few adjustments now and then. But caviar remained, making the difference between the haves and the have nots. No two ways about it. Even now that the sturgeons are disappearing from the Caspian Sea, there are still people who can afford Imperial Beluga, the very finest malossol from wild sturgeon, even though fishing it is banned. The wealthy purchase it by the bucket load, vats of the stuff: two pound tins, not those piddling two ounce numbers we sell to the nouveau riche. "Illegal, impossible to get hold of!" the Americans say. The Russians agree. The Iranians swear to it. Even the Chinese get huffy, because they're in on the act now too. But it's all nonsense, because if you've got the cash you can always get caviar. Like in the days of the Tsar. Like during the war. Like in my day.

I've retired now though. I've had everything I wanted in life, apart from ending the road with Rebecca. And this is the cross I now bear: the gaping hole she left, that has slowly filled up with memories, buried stuff from way back.

I even remembered the photograph that explained all of it. It was Lorenzo Cavicchi who showed it to me, the day I went to Ferrara to pay my condolences for Andrea and Enrico, both killed by the Germans.

"They died for freedom," their father said, without a tear.

"I should have joined the cause too," I told him awkwardly.

"That doesn't matter now, you're a good lad Nello Scaramagli, and that's what counts."

So I came out and asked him what had been on my mind since our first meeting:

"What does 'no gods, no masters' mean?"

Cavicchi senior smiled and murmured: "So you no longer hate your father."

"No, I don't hate him," I mumbled, looking at my shoes.

"Wait here," he said.

And he returned with a photograph - "Here you are."

He handed it to me. There were mountains in the background, and a lake, and in the foreground a group of young people, smiling at the photographer. They were all fairly well-dressed. I looked at it but I didn't understand at first.

"That's your father," he said, pointing to the youngest member of the group. A youngster with a shock of dark hair, light-colored eyes, like mine, I'd say, and a cocky attitude about him. He was wearing knickerbockers. He looked like he was ready to take on the world. Or maybe he was just young and stupid, like I was, with all those things I couldn't understand.

Standing beside him there was another lad, with fair hair, but older, almost a man, wearing a jacket, waistcoat and bow tie, with a waxed moustache and neatly done hair. Brylcreamed, it looked like. He was smoking a pipe, and had that faintly sad, dreamy air of Uncle about him... Uncle? It was Uncle! And to think I'd grown up believing my father and Uncle hated each other.

Another one, standing with one leg bent, impeccably dressed, with a beard, little glasses and a straw boater, was Mr. Cavicchi himself. He was jokily leaning on another guy in shirtsleeves with a half-unbuttoned waistcoat, a beret on his head, a cigar clamped between his teeth and a dark handlebar moustache... The Turk! It was him alright. Anyone would have recognized him, even just from that half smile of his.

Slightly in front of the others was a very beautiful woman, with her hair up. She was wearing a sort of coat while the others seemed to be dressed much lighter. I recognized her without a murmur: nothing could surprise me by then. It was the caviar lady. In her hand was a book, a book that I recognized. I figured it out for myself this time, as it was none other than the poetry of John Keats.

"We were all in love with Clara," said Cavicchi.

"Who?"

"Clara Macchioro."

That's how I found out the caviar lady's name.

"Was my father in love with her too?"

"Who? Menandro? No, he only had eyes for your mother."

Then I turned the photograph over. On the back was written Lausanne, 1914, and in big letters, no gods, no masters... I should have asked what they were all doing there in 1914, but I didn't. I thought, perhaps wrongly, that I'd got it all worked out. I looked at the photograph again: all five of them looked so strong, their expressions so focussed and determined, shining straight out of the picture. I was dumbstruck... Mr. Cavicchi realized and said: "We were young..."

He wanted me to keep the photograph, but I didn't take it. I didn't take it because I had decided to forget. To forget forever.

But now here I am, on December 27th 2007, frost covering the trees in crystals; here I am with a ticket in my hand, ready to board the old Littorina rail car. I thought no, I wouldn't go through with it, but then I thought: 'Just do it, what are you afraid of?' So I set off to see for myself. What, who knows? Well, I suppose to see whether anything was left of that world, our world, our century.

I took a seat, upholstered now, not like the wooden benches there used to be in third class. Because I always traveled in third class: I was the nephew, not the son of the stationmaster, as most people thought. I was not entitled to travel for free. Now I'm here, on a shabby but modern train, with my eyes glued to the window, just like when I was a boy. I watch the villages that lie along the Po slip past, one after the other, but you can't see the river from the train.

Today everything is frosty and white. Apparently they don't even get fog any more. That has gone, like the fishermen on the riverside, the pontoon bridges, the sturgeons. Like Nicola, back then. Like me and Bechi now.

I still remember when we almost collided in Milan, at the

university. I looked into those dark eyes, the same dark eyes I remembered from the day when I tried to help her clean our kitchen floor. And her, a woman of class, from a good family. She was in Milan because she'd been sent to study law. And she wasn't really the Turk's niece. It had been Clara Macchioro, the caviar lady, who convinced Uncle, and Uncle who convinced the Turk, to hide her among the fishermen. The racial laws had been passed and the lady had her head screwed on: she knew it was only going to get worse, and that Bechi wouldn't have survived if she'd stayed in the city.

When I think that I used to believe that it was the Jews who ruined the world, who brought down the Roman Empire and crucified Our Lord... And I believed it alright, when I went to visit Bechi wearing my black shirt. How was I to know that Jews could be dewy-eyed and cultured? I'd never seen one, and without realizing it I was falling in love. With a Jew, I mean. Actually I'd already fallen in love with one, because the caviar lady was Jewish and I admired her more than... more than Uncle, more than the Turk, more than anyone else I knew. It's taking me back, that's for sure. I sound like a child again, at the age of almost eighty.

Anyway the day I heard Bechi being called by her real name, I got the shock of my life. Her friend was calling her: "What's up with you? You look like you've seen a ghost. Rebecca, c'mon! Let's get a move on!"

"Rebecca?"

"I think we need to talk..."

So me and Bechi, and her friend, all went to have a hot chocolate, which at that time for me was the height of luxury. And she blurted it out. It didn't take me long to figure out the rest. So I worked up the courage and told her my secret.

"My real name is Nullo, not Nello, like I told everyone."

"What did you say your name was?" the friend asked.

Rebecca was laughing.

"Nullo, Nullo Scaramagli. It means Nobody. It's the name my father gave me before he went off and got killed with the anarchists in Spain. He gave me a name, but not a surname."

I couldn't look either of them in the eye, but then I felt Rebecca's light touch on my face.

"What are you doing? Everyone'll see you!" her friend hissed.

When I opened my eyes I saw that she'd kept her fiery spirit from the riverside years: she was sticking out her tongue, like a monkey, at her friend, who was all red in the face. Good on you Bechi. You've always been special, my love. I knew it the first time I set eyes on you. That's why I couldn't bear the idea of such a smart girl being there, in the Turk's house, leading that life. How on earth did you fall for Nicola? Couldn't you see what kind of future you would have had? Boiling up the laundry with wood ash, then beating it in the river, on your knees mopping up sturgeon blood, risking your life on a wooden boat in the river currents, or waiting at home, with a hungry brood, waiting to hear the cry that a whopper had been landed or receive the news that the fog had taken your man. But that's how it was. You were in love with Nicola. He told me he'd kissed you. And it was plain to see.

I don't recognize the villages I'm seeing through the train window. Even though it's the same journey I took to school every day. Every day on this very line. Who knows what Uncle would say if he could see all these derelict stations. I can't even seem to recognize any of them...

I get off at the village, but there's nothing there that reminds me of the places where I grew up. The station is new, brand new, with a proper foyer, but no stationmaster's office, not even a ticket office. Automatic glass doors. Remo's signal box on the other side of the tracks has gone too. There's nothing left. I look up and see that even my home has disappeared: the flat above the station where I lived as a boy - Mother's kitchen, the room where Uncle used to sleep after his night shifts, our lounge. The terrace where I used to look out over the countryside. Where I studied. Where I could watch the trains from above. Where they put the anti-aircraft guns towards the end of the war...

There's nothing left of my home. In its place is a pointed roof, as if it was a Greek temple and not a stupid station in a backwater by the Po. I don't know why I've come.

I look around. The road is different too, there's a roundabout, a square, I don't recognize any of it, and I can't even work out which way the village is. I ask at the coffee bar where I go to warm up. At my age you feel the cold more. I stir the froth on my cappuccino, messing it around, and wonder what's become of my old life, the station. All these questions are going round in my head, but suddenly I'm not even sure I can still speak Italian. In the end all I manage to do is ask the way to the village.

"You walking or taking the bus?"

"Walking."

"That way then."

On foot, of course. The station was only ever just outside

the village. I start walking, along the frost-covered fence by the railway line, lost in a swirl of memories I can't quite pin down. Here must have been where the railway workers' house was, and the villas would have been over there... But now there's nothing left. Just an empty road, and old me walking along. A few cars pass, going in the opposite direction, towards the station. I must be nearly at the village, they can hardly have moved that...

I never told anyone. Secrets are only secrets if you take them to your grave. What I didn't understand back then was that it was us, with our wars and our progress, killing the world. I'd thought it was just fate, chance. That's why, deep down, I was glad they'd killed Nicola. I've always been ashamed of that, but it's the truth.

It was when I ran into Bechi that day in Milan that I realized that that bullet was my good fortune. Or perhaps I should say *our* good fortune. For as much as we cared about Nicola, or thought we did, in all those years we never mentioned his name again. We buried him. Only when our son Andrea was born was I afraid that Bechi would want to call him Nicola. But she didn't.

We left him on there, on the riverside, and went looking for our own happiness. The guilt has always stayed with me, as if we'd killed him with our own hands, when all we did was bury the memory.

And, I suppose, or rather there's no supposing about it, I did nothing to find out who killed him. Because I had a suspicion that it was not a stray bullet, but a revenge killing on the very last day of the war, Remo taking his revenge on the Turk. An evil deed, with the war over, borne of the hatred and bitterness in Remo's heart. I don't know. That's what I thought, but I never actually tried to find out what really happened. There were little clues, sensations, hints dropped by Remo when he returned to the station after the amnesty for Fascists. I could have investigated, sleuthed a bit, tried to find out whether there was some element of truth in my suspicions. Or maybe it was the war that got me thinking badly of everyone, even someone who had nothing to do with it and was only trying to save his own skin. I don't know.

I do know that Nicola's death brought me relief rather than anger. That's what I've never told anyone, not even Rebecca. For a long time, in the early years, before I forgot, I told myself that it was fate that took Nicola, natural selection. Natural selection to save the best kind of people. And stupidly I counted myself among that number. But that kind of natural selection does not exist: no-one saved the sturgeon and the caviar, which have been gone from around these parts for half a century. In the Caspian Sea the sturgeons are destined to go so quickly that I might even see it in my own lifetime. The Turk was right: when humans meddle with things, they make a mess.

Rebecca, she was the key to it all. She'd chosen Nicola when she should have chosen me. In the end she married me, and she lived like a queen. But she was not happy.

I never had any regrets. After all, I was happy she had chosen me. It's taken me a lifetime to understand that a single moment, a single deed, can change the course of history, but that the new course is not necessarily better than what got left behind. I did everything I could to forget the past.

But now I'm here and I can see myself as a boy, on the riverside, that morning as day was breaking. I'd gone because it was time to end the war and we couldn't let those bastard Germans escape with their lives. Remo, and the Fascists like him, needed a lesson too. However far they ran, there was no way they could swim across the Po. At seventeen I was old enough to be part of that war, the war that had taken everything from us, even the very idea of who we were.

I'd gone to the riverside to ask the Turk and Nicola if they wanted to come and hunt down the krauts. Then when I got there I heard the shot. I turned around. Nicola's shout was muffled, more shock than pain. The Turk's scream ripped through the morning mist like a curtain being torn in two. I got scared and ran to the river. And then I saw. And I understood. And...

I look up at this icy December morning. These old legs make everything seem further away...

My God! It's the station! My station! Those bastards have moved the station, built a new one. No respect, not even for this. Our station, Uncle's station, is right here, boarded up with panels and padlocks, abandoned.

What I wouldn't give to breathe in the comforting aroma of Mother's minestrone soup, to hear the voices, the trains rattling through, and smell the fug of coal and fuel oil, the black smoke of the locomotives. To hear Uncle blowing his whistle, the telegraph tapping and the Lady waiting... There are the vegetable plots by the railwaymen's houses, and the... I sit on the bench by the first platform. It hasn't changed. I feel drunk... I feel... I...

I look around and everywhere I look there's a memory that comes to me like a scene in a movie. I get up and start walking again. Every step is harder than the last. Every time I blink there are different colors, smells, people. The years pass by, my life, I don't know...

And look over there! The tracks are half buried, the sleepers are piled up in a heap, the bumpers are rusty. Even the railings on the terrace of our house look like they're coming down...

The track is still there, I should have spotted it on my way here. You can still see the sign with the name of the village in white letters against a black background, over the entrance, where the ticket office used to be. I walk onto the platform. Now I recognize everything. Even the smells.

I can see Remo's house, the old signal box on the other side of the tracks. The windows are broken, the door is hanging off its hinges. What a lousy world we've left.

There's just one more thing I have to understand. One thing I have to see. Something that I have been too much of a coward all my life to do: to find out whether it was him, Remo, who killed my best friend. Because Nicola was not only the best friend I ever had, perhaps he was my only real friend. And I chose to forget him. I blocked him out, erased him from my memory. Only now, that Rebecca is gone, do I realize how much life is a useless race, a foolish attempt to get there first, leaving everything and everyone else behind. I try to climb up towards the tracks, slipping on the stones, but even one meter seems an impossible feat. It's the kind of effort where you have to stop for breath. On the first attempt my feet sink into the stones and I don't make it up the mound where the tracks are.

The gray sky looks threatening against the white frost, but I know that this is my station. And that is Remo's house. And that's where I have to look for answers. I'm old. And getting mixed up. And not very steady on my feet either. I'm ashamed to say it, but there it is. It's hard to know what's real and what is dreams and memories. I can feel the stones slipping and sliding under my feet.

"Nello, don't do it!"

I hear a strangled cry. It sounds like Rebecca's voice, but without the softness of time. It has an almost metallic edge, this distant order carried by the wind.

"Nullo, don't do it!"

This time it's my real name.

It's then that I see the white horse. I see it running towards me and it's turning into a sturgeon, an immense sturgeon. Then the train comes.

Index

The Caviar Lady

24580131R00134

Printed in Poland
by Amazon Fulfillment
Poland Sp. z o.o., Wrocław